Acclaim for *We All Want Impossible Things*:

'Remarkable . . . A whip-smart, funny, beautifully observed
and exquisitely characterised novel about how even
the deepest of losses can be accompanied by a joyous
affirmation of life.'
Observer

'I adored this book. Jubilant, devastating, tender, heartbreaking,
I found myself both in tears and "snorty-laughing". I know
it will be one of those novels I return to time and time again,
and recommend to everyone . . . A masterclass on friendship,
family love, memory, and the messiness of life and
love and dying. Pure genius.'
Rachel Joyce, author of *The Unlikely Pilgrimage of Harold Fry*

'Breezy New York Nora-Ephron-style wit meets hospice
memoir to create something profoundly beautiful . . . comforting,
so funny, moving but never mawkish and packed with all kinds
of love. It's one of my favourite books ever.'
Marian Keyes, author of *Again, Rachel*

'This is a proper laugh-out-loud tale of friendship that
will utterly win your heart . . . A truly special
book – prepare to read this, fall in love and then hector
everyone you know into reading it.'
Stylist

'Devastatingly funny . . . handled with compassion and
courage in elegant prose lightened by honest humour.'
Mail on Sunday

WE ALL
WANT
IMPOSSIBLE
THINGS

CATHERINE NEWMAN

PENGUIN BOOKS

TRANSWORLD PUBLISHERS
Penguin Random House, One Embassy Gardens,
8 Viaduct Gardens, London SW11 7BW
www.penguin.co.uk

Transworld is part of the Penguin Random House group of companies
whose addresses can be found at global.penguinrandomhouse.com

First published in Great Britain in 2022 by Doubleday
an imprint of Transworld Publishers
Penguin paperback edition published 2023

A CIP catalogue record for this book
is available from the British Library.

ISBN
9781529177220

Printed and bound in Great Britain by Clays Ltd, Elcograf S.p.A.

The authorized representative in the EEA is Penguin Random House Ireland,
Morrison Chambers, 32 Nassau Street, Dublin D02 YH68.

Penguin Random House is committed to a sustainable future
for our business, our readers and our planet. This book is made
from Forest Stewardship Council® certified paper.

FOR ALI POMEROY, 1968–2015
BRIGHTEST STAR, MOST MISSED.

And February was so long that it lasted into March.

—*Dar Williams, "February"*

WE ALL
WANT
IMPOSSIBLE
THINGS

PROLOGUE

"Edi. Are you sleeping?"

I'm whispering, even though the point is to wake her up. Her eyelids look bruised, and her lips are pale and peeling, but still she's so gorgeous I could bite her face. Her dark hair is growing back in. "Wake up, my little chickadee," I whisper, but she doesn't stir. I look at Jude, her husband, who shrugs, runs an open palm over his handsome, exhausted face.

"Edichka," I say a little louder, Slavically. She opens her eyes, squinches them shut again, then snaps them back open, focuses on my face, and smiles. "Hey, sweetheart," she says. "What's up?"

I smile back. "Oh, nothing," I say. *A lie!* "Jude and I were just making some plans for you."

"Plans like banh mi from that good banh mi place?" she says. "I'm starving." She rubs her stomach over her johnny. "No. Not starving. Not even hungry, actually. I just want to taste something tasty, I guess." She tries to sit up a little and then remembers the remote, and the top of her bed rises with the mechanical whirring that would be on my Sloan Kettering soundtrack mixtape, if I made one. Also the didgeridoo groaning of the guy in the room next door. The sunny

1

lunch-tray person saying, "Just what the doctor ordered!" even when it's weirdly unwholesome "clear liquids" like black coffee and sugar-free Jell-O.

"Banh mi can definitely be arranged," I say. I'm stalling, and Jude sighs. He pulls a chair over by her head, sits in it.

"Awesome," Edi says. She fishes a menu from the stack crammed into her bedside drawer. "Extra spicy mayo. No daikon."

"Edi," I say. "I have been madly in love with you for forty-two years. Am I going to suddenly forget your abiding hatred of radishes?"

She smiles dotingly at me, flutters her eyelashes.

"Wait," I say. "*Extra* spicy mayo? Or extra-spicy *mayo*?"

She says, "What?" and Jude says, "Edi." She hears it in his voice, turns to him and says, "What?" again, but I'm already starting to cry a little bit.

"Shit," she says. "No, no. You guys." She wrings her hands. "I'm not ready for this. Whatever this is. What is this?"

Here's what this is: Out in the hallway, Jude had asked about Edi's treatment. "Isn't she supposed to get her infusion today?" he'd said, and the nurse had said cheerfully, "Nope! We're all done with that." And so, it seemed, we were. Nobody exactly talked to us about this decision. It was like it had already happened, in some other time and place. You order a burger and the kitchen makes an executive decision in the back. "We're out of burgers," your server says. "There's just this plate of nothing with a side of morphine and grief."

Ellen, the social worker, had taken Jude and me into her office to give us a *make the most of her remaining days* talk—while simultaneously clarifying that this most-making would need to happen *not there*. We were confused. "I'm confused," I said, and Ellen had nodded slowly, crinkled her eyes into a pitying smile, and handed us a pamphlet called "Next Steps, Best Steps." It was about palliative care.

Hospice. "But these are the *worst* steps," I said, because apparently nothing is too obvious for me to mention, and Ellen passed me a box of tissues. "I feel like I'm mad at you, but also like this might not be your fault," I said, truthfully, and she laughed and said, "I promise you I understand." I liked her after that.

Ellen tried to help us figure out what to do. Edi and Jude's son, Dashiell, is seven and has already spent three of those years living with his mom's illness. Ellen wondered if bringing her home for hospice care might simply be too traumatizing, and suggested that inpatient care might be a better option, given the likelihood of a swift and harrowing end-of-life scenario. This seemed not unsensible. Dash's last visit had been a disaster: when Edi bent to kiss him good-bye, blood had poured out of her nose and terrified him. It had just been a garden-variety nosebleed, it turned out, but Dash, already fragile, was stained. Literally stained. Figuratively scarred. "You might even have him say good-bye to her sooner than later," Ellen offered. "So that he isn't worrying about when it's coming."

"When what's coming?" I said. The inevitability of Edi's death was like a crumpled dollar bill my brain kept spitting back out. "Sorry," I said a second later. "I understand."

We called the recommended hospices from the hospital lobby, but they all had a wait list. "A wait list?" Jude had said. "Do they understand the premise of hospice?" We pictured an intake coordinator making endless calls, crossing name after name off her list. "Yes, yes. I see. Maybe next time!"

"Sloan says she's got to be out by tomorrow midday," Jude said, and passed me the cigarette we were splitting. We were not the only people huddled in our puffy jackets outside the famous cancer hospital, exhaling our stupidly robust good health away into the January cold, where clouds of smoke should have been gathering to form the words *We're so fucked*.

"There's a hospice up by us," I said, and Jude looked at me unblinkingly for a few beats. I live in Western Massachusetts. He ground the butt under his heel, picked it up, and tossed it into a trash can. "It's nice," I said. "I've visited people there. It's an actual house."

"And?" he said.

I didn't know. "I don't know," I said. "Would that be crazy? To bring her up there? I mean, they're saying a week or two, maybe even less."

"What would we do?" Jude said. "I really don't want to take Dash out of school."

"Yeah, no," I said. "Don't do that."

"But I can't leave him. Not now."

"I know." My hair was stuck in the zipper of my jacket, but I didn't bother trying to get it out. My eyes were watering from smoke and cold and also from the crying I seemed to be doing.

"I don't understand what you're saying, Ash."

"I know. I guess I'm not sure what I'm saying," I said.

"Would Dash and I say good-bye to her *here*?"

"I don't know," I said. "Could you?"

"I don't know," he said. "I mean, you were at our *wedding*, Ash. 'Til death do us part. I can't really imagine leaving her now—who I'd even be if I did that."

"Jude." I leaned forward to touch my forehead to his. "You wouldn't be leaving her. You'd be sparing your child. Edi's child. You've done 'in sickness and health' truly magnificently. We'd just be"—What? What would we be?—"seeing her off in stages. Tag-teaming it."

"It's kind of your dream," Jude teased. "Getting her all to yourself."

"I know!" I said. "I mean, finally!"

"You can be her knight in shining armor like you've always

wanted." He laughed, not unkindly. Does he love me? Yes. Do I drive him crazy? Also yes. But it was true that I'd felt stuck away up in New England, happy enough in my life there but wishing I were still in New York with everybody I'd grown up with, guiltily wishing I were closer to Edi. Now my daughters were mostly grown, and also my husband seemed to have left me. I was in the perfect place in my life at the perfect time of Edi's. Not perfect in the normal sense, obviously.

"You've always accused me of being an opportunist," I said to Jude, and he said, "True."

We cried a little more, our puffy arms wrapped around each other's necks and heads. Then Jude retrieved a bottle of lavender hand sanitizer from his coat pocket, gestured at me to hold out my hands, sprayed them, sprayed his own, misted his hair for good measure. I shook a couple of Tic-Tacs into his palm and mine, and we went fragrantly back in through the revolving door to wake Edi up and ask her something we hadn't even finished figuring out. The worst question in the whole entire world, as it turned out.

CHAPTER 1

At least I'm not sleeping with the hospice music therapist.

Cedar. He's twenty years old, twenty-five tops, and he has a voice like an angel who maybe swallowed a bag of gravel. His guitar case is covered in stickers: a smiley face, a skull, Drake, Joni Mitchell. "When you're famous, I'm going to say I knew you when!" I said once, and it was a mistake. He shook his head, his baby forehead suddenly crosshatched with distress. I'd gotten him so wrong. "No, no," he said. "This is it. I'm already doing the thing I want to do."

"Of course!" I said quickly. "It's such a perfect job for you." And he said, "Yeah, though sometimes I dream that somebody requests something, and I'm like, 'Hang on a sec, I don't know that one. Let me just look it up on my phone.' But while I'm googling 'Luck Be a Lady' or whatever, they die. And that's the last thing anyone ever said to them. 'Hang on a sec.'"

"Shit, Cedar," I said, and he said, "Right?"

Now he's sitting on the end of the bed, strumming the beginning of something. The Beatles, "Across the Universe." Edi's eyes are closed, but she smiles. She's awake in there somewhere. "Cedar," she says, and he says, "Hey, Edi," lays a palm on her shin, then returns

7

to his song, strumming some and singing, humming the parts he can't remember. My heart fills with, and releases, grief in time to my breathing.

We've been—*Edi's* been—at the Graceful Shepherd Hospice for three weeks now. Three weeks is a long time at hospice, but also, because of what hospice means, it kind of flies by. But it flies by crawlingly, like a funhouse time warp. Like life with a newborn: It's breakfast, all milk and sunshine, and then it's feeding and changing that recur forever, on a loop, like some weird *soiled nighties* circle of hell. And then somehow it's the next day again, and you're like, "Who's hungry for their breakfast?" Only *nobody* is hungry for their breakfast. Except Edi. "Oooh. Make me French toast?" she said this morning to Olga, the Ukrainian nurse we love, who responded, "Af *khorse*."

The hospice had estimated, when we checked her in, that Edi would be their *guest* for just a week or two. "We don't think of this as a place where people come to die," the gravely cheerful intake counselor had said to us. "We think of it as a place where people come to *live*!" "To live *dyingly*," Edi had whispered to me, and I'd laughed. We all refer to the hospice as Shapely—as in, "I'll meet you over at Shapely"—because Edi, only half-awake when we were first talking about it, thought it was called the Shapely Shepherd. "Like a milkmaid in one of those lace-up outfits?" she'd said, and I'd said, "Wait. What?" And then, when I pictured what she was picturing, "Yes. Exactly like that."

Hospice is a complicated place to pass the time because you are kind of officially dying. "Am I, though?" Edi says sometimes, when dying comes up, as it is wont to come up in hospice, and I pull my eyebrows up and shrug, like *Who knows?* "If anything happens to me . . ." she likes to start some sentences—about Dash or Jude or her journals or her jewelry. And I say, "What on earth would happen to you?" and she laughs and says, "I know, right? But just on the off chance."

Sometimes the hospice physician comes through—the enormous, handsome man we call Dr. Soprano because he looks like James Gandolfini—and she says, "When do you think I can get out of here?" You can tell that he can't tell if she's kidding or not, probably because she's not really kidding. "Good question," he says, poker-faced, rummaging through her box of edibles and breaking off a tiny nibble of the chocolate kind he likes. "Do you mind?" he says, after the fact, and then, "If anyone's getting out of here, Edi, it is definitely you."

Which, to be honest, is not saying much. The average age of the other patients is a hundred and fifty. They're so old, some of these folks, their bodies so worn down and used up, that sometimes when you peek into their rooms to say hi you can't even tell if they're there in their beds or not. They're nearly completely flat, like paper dolls, with just a tiny fluff of cotton glued at the top for hair. You half expect to see a ghost climb up out of their body, like in a cartoon. One of them likes me to come in and hold her hand. She always offers me a lemon drop from her special tin and says, "Did you come straight off the school bus?" And I say, "I did, Ruth! I came right to you." Forty-five-year-old me, fresh off the school bus with my under-eye bags and plantar fasciitis and boobs hanging down my torso like beige knee socks with no legs in them. There's nothing like hospice to remind you that decrepitude is totally relative.

"I believe I may be mildly *demented*," Ruth whispered once, apologetically, and I was like, "Oh, please. Same."

Ruth has been here for over a year, which I know is a total inspiration to Edi, although she has never mentioned it. Ruth is also the person who watches *Fiddler on the Roof* every afternoon and also some nights. The volume is turned way up and, for hours every day, it's the soundtrack of everybody's dying. You're helping someone into compression stockings or fresh briefs during "Matchmaker." Someone is weeping in your arms while Tevye yiddle-diddles "If I Were a Rich Man." It's "Sunrise, Sunset," only you're cry-laughing because there's a turd on the floor and you don't know if it's human or from one of the resident dogs.

Now we hear the overture starting up, Ruth clapping in delight, whooping from her room, and Cedar says, "That's my cue," and zips his guitar into its case. He kisses Edi's cheek, kisses mine, and closes the door gently on his way out.

"Oh my god, Ash," Edi says. Her eyes are still closed. "You're sleeping with Cedar."

"Edi! Jesus. I'm not a grave robber."

She laughs and says, "I think you mean *cradle* robber."

"Ugh," I say, and palm my forehead. "Yes, sorry." There are many hidden awkwardnesses in hospice, like when you say things like "This gelato is so good I'm dying," or "Oof, I ate too much gelato, kill me," and then remember that there's an actually dying person also eating the gelato, or a person who might genuinely wish you would kill them. "He's so cute, though," I add. "Timothée Chalamet would play him in the movie." She smiles, wags a finger at me in warning.

"Don't," she says, and I mean it when I say, "I would seriously never."

"Hey," she says, her eyes still closed. "Honey's coming over in a little. I hope that's cool with you. He's bringing me some stuff." Honey is my ex-husband. Or he would be, if we weren't too cheap and lazy to get an actual divorce. The *stuff* he brings Edi is from the dispensary in town, which he owns. Or, I guess, which *we* own, technically.

"Of course," I say. "He's practically living at the house again. I think he's coming by later, to see Jonah."

"Wait," she says, "Jonah's still here?"

"*Here* here?" I'm not always sure how much she's following. "Like in the room? No," I say.

"No," she says, and opens her eyes. "I know that. Here in town." Her brother comes up from New York on the weekends, and he's usually gone by Monday. But he's staying an extra couple of days this week, telecommuting from my house to squeeze in a few more visits at Shapely.

"Yeah," I say. "He came by this morning. But maybe you were kind of out of it? From the meds." She nods, shakes her head, pissed. She doesn't remember.

"Fuuuuuck," she says. "This suuuuucks."

I picture her mind like a bar, her thoughts and memories nursing their last round. It's closing time, and you don't have to go home, but you can't stay here. I untangle her tubes and wires, hang them on the pole behind her, and climb into her bed. A few little tears drip out of her eyes, which are closed again. "It does," I say, laying my head on her pillow. I touch a tear with my fingertip, touch my fingertip to my lips. "It totally sucks."

CHAPTER 2

Jonah and I are talking about what we always talk about, which is inventions that would save Edi's life. You hear all the time about people dying of cancer, and it makes some kind of sense if you don't think about it too much. Until Edi, though, I had never really wondered about what they died *of*. Because it's not actually an abstraction that kills anybody—the word *cancer*, or the fact of cancer, coming at them, yodeling, with a raised hatchet. It's the breakdown of bodies, of their specific organs and functions.

Edi, like most people with ovarian cancer, will die—*if* she dies!—because her guts stopped working. What will kill her, ultimately, is (spoiler alert) bowel obstruction and malabsorption, catastrophic electrolyte imbalance and then kidney or liver failure. "It's just fixing a broken pump," Jonah is saying to me. "Jesus. You practically expect them to have an app for that."

"I want to put it to the fancy engineering kids at MIT," I say. "Can't I just send an email? 'Contest alert! Invent a pacemaker, but for intestines instead of a heart! Win a bubble-tea gift card!'"

"Yeah," Jonah says. "You could ask Jules." Jules, my older

daughter, is a fancy engineering sophomore at MIT. "It might be kind of a lot of pressure, though," he adds, and I say, "True," and sigh.

Jonah, the sighingest person I know, sighs too—he would never leave my sigh hanging unanswered—and rolls nudely onto his back. "Edi's going to kill us," he says, like he said when we were teenagers, and I say, like I said when we were teenagers, "Not if she doesn't find out."

Jelly the cat climbs up onto Jonah's chest and peers into his face unblinkingly. "She made some unsettling eye contact with me earlier," Jonah says.

"Yeah," I say. "You grunting around in here is not her favorite. If she had fingers, she would have flipped you off."

The doorknob rattles, and we yank the sheet up to our chins, the cat flying off the bed, just as Belle, my seventeen-year-old, bursts in. She stops short in the doorway. "Oh my god, Mom, could you be any grosser?" she says, then adds, "No offense, Jonah," and he says, "None taken."

"Don't slut-shame me," I say, and she laughs, says, "Fair," and hands me a permission slip to sign. I sit up carefully, keeping the sheet wound around my tragic boobs so as to not depress her further.

"Didn't you already take a field trip to the wastewater treatment plant in, like, fifth grade?" I say, and she shrugs, says, "I'm just looking forward to napping on the bus," snatches the paper out of my hands, scoops Jelly up, and is out the door again, yelling back to us, "Dinner in twenty. Enchiladas. Don't forget Dad's coming. Maybe lock your fucking *door*."

"Thanks!" I yell after her, and then grimace at Jonah.

"Awkward," he says, and I say, "Truth."

"Do you think I'm a bad mom?" I say, and Jonah rolls back onto his side to smile at me.

"Maybe?"

I can hear Belle clanging around the kitchen, and I can't tell if it's normal clanging—the unavoidable sound of the colander hitting the sink—or if it's pointed *my mom is a gruesome skank* clanging. But the ceiling of my bedroom is slanted and low, and it's cozy in here, and the smell of cumin wafts in to console me.

"Oh well," is all I say, and Jonah laughs.

I've been friends with Jonah as long as I've been friends with Edi, since Edi and I were assigned, in nursery school, to take care of Vinnie, the classroom Venus flytrap. We fed Vinnie bites of bologna from our sandwiches and sang him the Jewish folk song "Dona, Dona" with so much tremulous vibrato that we actually made ourselves cry. The traps swelled with lunch meat, turned black, and fell off, and one day we came in and Vinnie was gone. There was a jade plant in his spot on the windowsill. "Only water for this one," our nice teacher said, and by then I had already gone to Edi's house and met her barky German shepherd, Zeus, and her dark-haired older brother, Jonah, and I'd fallen in love with everyone.

I lucked out into getting a big brother along with a best friend. The kind of brother you end up boning, sure, but there were many, many chaste years before that, I swear. It was all Connect Four and *Gilligan's Island*. It was fifty-cent pizza slices and fifty-cent Sabrett hot dogs, sixteen-cent Chuckles candy and the complete first eight series of Wacky Pack trading cards, with their wintergreen bubblegum smell. I never even thought to look at Jonah back then. I'm lying! I had a huge crush on him, the whole entire time—and, yeah, I'd sometimes catch Edi looking at me funny. But we were a happy trio nonetheless, and our *don't ask, don't tell* method of shadiness and stealth worked well for us through many decades.

Now Jonah has no hair on his head, but his thick, luscious eyebrows shine auburnly in the last of the light. "Your eyebrows," I say admiringly, and he runs a finger over one, waggles them suggestively, says, "You like?" and then heaves himself up to sitting, bends this way and that to crack his back. "It's a lot for the old bod, spending time with you," he says, before gathering up, and stepping back into, his assorted expensive clothing.

He manages a hedge fund, and I have never bothered to actually learn what that means, aside from, I assume, stealing from the poor. I always picture an actual hedge—a topiary shaped like a dollar sign, Jonah going at it with a Weedwacker, heavy bags of money falling on him from a cloudless sky. I describe this to him now, and he says, "It's exactly like that," then gestures at his gray cashmere sweater, his fancy jeans, says, "All this could be yours one day." I pull on the raggedy My Little Pony hoodie I stole from Belle, say, "One day very soon, since I'm hiding it all before you leave."

Downstairs, Belle is making one of her trademark salads, lots of sturdy, difficult vegetables lined up on the cutting board. "Winter in New England," she likes to say piously, "is not a time for lettuce." Rather, it's a time, it would seem, for enormous radishes and dirty rutabagas and purple-topped turnips, everything scrubbed and shredded and dressed sharp with lemon and chiles, all of it surprisingly, bracingly delicious.

"What can I do?" I say, "Besides lighting the candles?"

She asks me to spoon sour cream into a bowl, to clean and chop a handful of cilantro, to warm four plates in the microwave, which I do. The window over our kitchen table still holds a sliver of pale pink daylight beneath the dark blue of evening, and I point this out to Belle. "Mom," she says, her hands massaging root vegetables in the giant wooden salad bowl, "can we please not have our millionth *It's February and the days are really getting longer!* conversation of the week? Yes, the days are getting longer."

"Sorry to be cheerful," I say, and she flips me off, before pulling on oven mitts to retrieve the enchiladas, which smell so good I'm actually dying. (Not *actually*, though!) I'm hungry, I realize. It's possible I haven't eaten all day.

"You are a perfect daughter," I say truthfully, and kiss Belle's temple with its dark fuzz of buzzed hair, and she squirms out of my grasp, smiles, and says, "Thanks."

Belle gets her kitchen talent from her dad, who did all the cooking before he left. He still does some of it here, even now, but he no longer runs the catering business he had for most of our marriage. What that business meant, besides the making of money, was that I drove carpool in a van with BAT OUT OF HELL'S KITCHEN stenciled flamingly on its side (he later changed the name to the friendlier Delish). And also that the bulk of our meals were composed of wedding and bar mitzvah leftovers.

The kids grew up imagining that fancy hors d'oeuvres were just regular food. "What even is that?" a fellow kindergartner once asked Jules about her mysterious lunch-box contents, and, according to the teacher, Jules had replied, "Stuffed portobello caps." "Stuffed with *what*?" the kid asked, and Jules squinted at the mushroom in her little hand before shrugging and saying, "Rosemary-scented focaccia?" "All endive, all the time," was a Honey mantra in those days, and the kids scooped up trout mousse or cranberry-studded goat cheese with the sweetly bitter leaves, because that's what there was. They ate smoked scallops as an after-school snack, poking them up with toothpicks, dragging them through horseradish aioli, and *mmmm*ing appreciatively. Food-wise, we were lucky. Maybe otherwise too, to be honest.

Now Jonah thumps down the stairs in his socks just as Honey is opening the kitchen door with a rush of cold air. "This was on the doorstep," he says, and passes me a delivery box. It's the metal pitcher I ordered for Edi's room. She's so thirsty all the time, and I'm too lazy to fill her cup from the kitchen as often as is required. A piece of paper labeled ASSEMBLY INSTRUCTIONS flutters from the box, and I pick it up, while Jonah and Honey embrace and Belle leans over my shoulder to look. The instructions consist only of an illustration of the pitcher, with an arrow pointing to it. Belle laughs. "That's the queerest!" She's already reclaimed the word *queer* to describe her own sexuality—but now she also seems to be *re*-reclaiming it for everyday exclamatory use. She magnets the paper to the fridge, puts the Indigo Girls on Spotify, and ushers everyone to the table.

The enchiladas are dark red, fragrant and spicy and delicious, cheese oozing out of them and pooling into the pinto beans, which Belle has simmered with bay leaves and onion. "This is amazing," I say, and Jonah and Honey agree. I love the people at the table so much, and the food is so good, and Edi is so sick, and I miss Jules, even though she's only an hour and a half away. Plus, the lovely, changing light! My poor marriage! The red wine, the candle glow, "Galileo" seeping out of the speaker. I could just cry.

"I could just cry," I say, and everyone nods, because probably I *will* cry, and nobody is overly surprised by this turn of events.

Belle pats my arm, says, "You're okay," like you'd say while you were putting a Band-Aid on a weepy small someone's invisible paper cut, and I laugh.

Honey catches us up on Edi, as is our habit these days: Whoever's been with her most recently has to tell everyone else every single thing they heard or noticed. There's not a ton. She looked tired, Honey notes, somewhat redundantly. She wanted to sit in the chair by the window, but after she tried swinging her legs over the side of the bed, she changed her mind and lay back down. She ate a few bites of minestrone, which Olga referred to as *noodle borscht*. They watched the minestrone exit her palliative venting gastrostomy—the PEG tube—which drains her stomach contents so she doesn't end up barfing (watching the PEG tube is the new *Naked and Afraid*, as Jonah likes to say). They changed her PICC line. She ate a THC gummy. She talked to Dash and Jude. She cried about Dash. She slept.

"Sorry, sweetie," Honey says, turning to Belle. I feel that way too. It's a lot to ask of a teenager, to listen to a conversation that's somehow incredibly dull but also really sad at the same time, like someone is telling you about a game of golf they played in a dream, but also Mozart's Requiem is playing.

"Please," Belle says. "What are we going to talk about? Porcupines eating corn on the cob? I'm good. It's all good."

"I mean, not *all*, obviously," she adds.

Jonah stands up, steps into his expensively robust winter boots—he's going to Shapely for a little—and I clear the table while Belle puts the leftover enchiladas in a Tupperware. "Take these to Edi, okay?" she says to Jonah, and he says, "Thank you. She'll love that."

Honey asks Belle if she wants to play a game before he leaves. "Dutch Blitz?" he says. "Yahtzee? Jacks?"

"I'm good, Dad, but thank you. I should probably do my calculus homework." She kisses his cheek and disappears upstairs. She is unfailingly sweet with Honey, which I appreciate. It seems fair, somehow, that she saves me all her spitfire and claws and tornadoes. The poisonous cobras and rotting Halloween pumpkins and shouty talkshow guests of her soul. Wait. *Does* it seem fair? I'm not actually sure.

Honey asks me if I want him to go or stay, and I tell him that I just want to not make any more decisions, so he pours each of us a fresh glass of wine and we sit together on the kitchen couch. Jelly headbutts his chin like a goat, then curls into his lap, and our other cat, Thumper, sprawls out next to him, tummy up. Honey strokes the cats and sings to them a little—Bob Marley's "One Love," only he swaps in the word *cat* for *love*.

There's some silver glinting in Honey's dark hair, which is falling into his eyes, and some more along his jaw, in the day's-end scruff of his beard. He still wears the tiny silver hoop earring I gave him when we were first dating. He still wears his wedding ring. My love for him feels like a cramp under my ribs. "This was my home for so long," he says simply, slightly amazed, like something you might announce from the car as you were driving through your old neighborhood, and I say, "It still is, Hon," even though it actually isn't still.

"I'm sorry," I say, and he says, "It is what it is," and takes my hand in his—his big, warm, familiar hand—and rests them both on top of the cat.

"I'm always here," he says. And he could mean here in his old house, which is true—he's here all the time. Or he could mean here, available to me still, in all of the marriage ways, which is also true.

"I know," I say. "But I'm so tired." And his voice is thick, but all he says is, "Ashley."

CHAPTER 3

Cedar steps into Edi's room, says, "Oh my goodness! Excuse me!" and backs out, pulling the door closed. Edi and I say simultaneous versions of, "No, no, you're fine! Come in! We're done." I've got a headlamp on, and I'm squatting over Edi in the bed, my knees on either side of her so that I can pluck out her chin hairs, but now I launch myself off the bed, pop the tweezers in my bag, and pull up a chair.

Sleet is sheeting grayly out the window, and Cedar's hair is soaked. I have a sneaking suspicion that he rode his bike over, but I'm trying not to treat him like he's one of my kids, so I don't ask. A pancakey smell wafts in from the kitchen. A pair of volunteers is making breakfast for everyone here who's still eating. It's afternoon, but nobody's too picky about what counts as morning or lunch or nighttime or, really, time in general.

"Any requests?" Cedar says, pulling his guitar from its case, and Edi scooches herself up in the bed a little, pushes her hair out of her face, and says, "Ooooh. This is a long shot. But do you know 'April Come She Will'?"

"I don't," Cedar says, "but I can totally google it." He catches my eye, and I pantomime a *The Scream* face, and he looks away quickly, smiling, pulls his phone from his pocket. "Simon and Garfunkel. Got it," he says, and fingers the guitar part for a minute, then sings it for us, stopping every little while to scroll through the lyrics.

I'm having a memory of being over at Edi's when we were ten, playing with our matching Snoopy stuffed animals—they were sick or getting married or maybe both—and Jonah was suddenly in the doorway. He was so handsome in his alligator shirt and smudge of mustache, holding a tape recorder. He was also furious. "Did you do this?" he asked, and pressed PLAY, and we heard him chant briefly in cracking Hebrew—*Barukh ata Adonai, eloheinu melekh ha-olam*—before it cut out and we heard Edi soulfully singing "Maybe" from *Annie*. "Did you record yourself singing over my haftorah practice tape?" Edi looked him in the eye, levelly, and said, "I did not."

Cedar plays for Edi while I catch up on my phone. There's a robocall from Belle's school, alerting me to her absence. "SOMEBODY HAIRBALLED ON THE COUCH," Belle herself has texted, and I write her back that if she were at school, where she is supposed to be, this would not be her problem to deal with. "Why aren't you at school?" I add, and she sends me an ambiguous halo emoji.

"New idea: a restaurant called Potassium!" Jonah has written. Recently, Edi's potassium levels have been perilously low. "The menu is clams and bananas and raisins." "Good idea," I text now, and Jonah writes back immediately, "Potassium!"

Edi's dad has texted from his condo in Florida. "Text me if there's an emergency," he has written. "Do you know what hospice is?" I text, then delete. "An emergency *at the hospice*? Like a fire?" I text, then delete. "Okay," I text and hit SEND.

"What the fuck is shiplap?" Belle texts, and I tell her to turn off HGTV and go back to school. *At least she's watching the actual television!* I think, which is weird.

Her sister, meanwhile, has texted me some miscellaneous hearts.

"Just thinking about you," she's written, and I send her back a long string of x's and o's.

"Hey, Jude," I text, like I like to, and Jude texts me back the eye-rolling emoji.

Edi dozes, then falls fully asleep while Cedar plays the David Bowie song "Heroes." This is one of Edi's absolute favorites. After her first surgery, I made her a banner that said, WE CAN BE HEROES, each letter stuck to a little paper flag, and she hung it in her hospital room. "*Debulking?*" she'd said about the surgical procedure to remove her tumor. "Seriously? They're, like, what? Taking a little off the top? It's not the *most* optimistic name." We were trying to understand, then, what her life was about to become. I think we're still trying to understand.

I creep out of the room with Cedar when he's done. Olga's in the hallway, and she holds up a pair of scissors when she sees me. "You do grooming. You can do this?" she says, and I say, "I can! I mean, probably, whatever it is."

"Cut *khairs?*" she says, and I say, "Yours?" and she laughs, runs a hand protectively over her stylish blond helmet, says, "No. No! Junior. For party."

"Sure," I say. "Happily." What I should probably really do is sneak home and get back to work, but I had a Ukrainian grandmother, so I need Olga to like me best. Well, Olga and every other person in the world.

"Come," she says. I follow her two doors down, where Junior sits in a wheelchair by his window, watching the cardinals at the feeder outside. Like Ruth, Junior has been here for over a year. "He's technically dying," Dr. Soprano explained to me. "But his insurance company wouldn't mind if he, you know, applied himself to that project a little more rigorously." Today, there's a balloon tied to his chair, and a glittery tiara perched on his head. His blue button-down shirt is pressed and crisp, tucked neatly into his pajama bottoms.

"Hi, Junior," I say. "It's Ash. Edi's friend. Is it your birthday? Happy birthday!"

"Happy birthday to you too," he says, and Olga says, "He is *khundred* today."

"A hundred!" I say, and Junior says, "A hundred what?"

"A hundred years old."

"You're not!" he says. "You can't be!"

I laugh. "You," I say, and he says, "Me what?" and I say, "Are getting a haircut."

"Yes," Junior says. "Just a little trim, if you would. Just to neaten it up a hair."

"A *hair*!" I say, laughing, and he says, "Yes." Kill me.

It would be hard to underestimate the amount of hair on Junior's head. It's like the down of a little baby chick, but a little baby chick with a crew cut and also alopecia. "Hang on," I say, and pop out to grab a blanket from the warmer, which I snap open and drape over his shoulders with a bit of flourish. I remove his birthday crown gently. Under my fingers, his hair feels like cobwebs, like fog. It is barely even a physical substance. Junior smiles, says, "If I'd known you were coming, I'd have put my teeth in."

"Please," I say. "Teeth are totally overrated."

I snip very delicately, taking care not to lop off one of his pale, papery ears. "How long have you been a lady barber?" he says, and I say, "Not long at all! I mean, except for the lady part. But I'm picking it up quickly." I make a big production of touching up the sides. When I wheel him over to the mirror to look, he squints, touches his head. "What do you think?" I say, and he says, "About what?"

"I don't know. Anything, I guess."

He says, "Smile and the world smiles with you," then beams at me

24

in the mirror, his mouth a merry cave filled entirely with the absence of his dentures.

Olga returns, says, "Nice *khairs* cut! Like real *saloon*! I get broom." I look at the floor, where, scattered about, there is approximately one quarter-teaspoon of fluff. I picture gathering it in my fingertips, popping it into an envelope, and mailing it to Locks of Love. *You're welcome!* the accompanying note could say. *Don't use it all in one place! Ha ha ha!*

"My wallet's on the dresser," Junior says, and I say, "This one's on the house. For your birthday." He thanks me, blows a kiss, waves good-bye.

I peek in on Edi, and her eyes are closed, but she's moaning. I sit on the edge of her bed. "Eds," I whisper. "Are you okay?"

"Yeah," she says. "I'm good." She moans some more.

"But are you *moaning*?" I say, and she says, "Am I?" Then, sheepish, "Yeah."

"Does something hurt?" I ask.

She moans, says, "Not really," and opens her eyes.

Even in hospice, with her teeth getting bigger by the day while the rest of her face seems to be evaporating, Edi looks like an Italian movie star: dark eyes, dark eyebrows, and a smile that's probably dazzling people two towns away—like, they're probably putting a protective hand up to their face, wondering about the glare, and it's Edi's smile. She's wearing an old Talking Heads T-shirt of Jonah's, and her collarbones jut over the top of it like, well, like *bones*. I assume it's not a coincidence that the closer people get to death, the more you see the extent to which we're all just skeletons in elaborate, fleshy waiting rooms.

She's not smiling now, though. "I'm worried that I shouldn't have come," she says.

"To Shapely?" I say.

"Yeah."

I nod.

"I should be in Brooklyn." That's where Jude and Dash are. It's where Edi lives. Lived? Lives. *Lived*.

"Tell me," I say, and she shakes her head, cries a little.

Suggesting that she move up here had gone about as badly as you probably imagine. Edi had cried and cried—first at the mention of hospice, then at the idea of leaving Dash. "I can't do that," she'd said. "I won't." We'd nodded, said, "Of course, okay," sat stunned and despairing while she drifted in and out of sleep. "We need to be making a plan B," Jude said, and I said, "I know." But we didn't. It had gotten late, eventually. Jude was dozing, and I gathered my things to go.

Jude was awake again. "Hey, take a taxi to your parents' apartment, okay?" he said, and I said, "Okay."

"Ash," he said wearily, and I said, "What?"

"Are you actually going to take the subway?"

Of course I was going to take the subway! Who was I, Bill Gates?

Edi opened her eyes too and said, "Okay," resolute. She was not talking about my mode of transportation. She drank a miniature can of apple juice in one swallow and said, "Bring Dash tomorrow and then I'll go. Do not talk to me about it." And so we held her quietly. We held her while the biggest loss of her life—which was bigger than the loss of her actual life—sank into her like mercury.

"Dash has a cold," Edi says now. I'd already heard this from Jude, who'd texted me a photo of Dash with his little red nose and a comically exaggerated frown.

"Poor Snufflekins," I say, and Edi shakes her head again. *No*.

"I'm not *there*," she says. "I'm not there to scramble his egg or kiss his forehead. My baby. I'm not *going to be there*. The whole rest of his life he's going to be sick without me. How can that be?" Her face collapses, and she cries and cries. I'm leaning awkwardly over the bed, trying to hold her and also getting snot in her hair.

"All of that caretaking," I say. I lean back so I can look at her. I'm crying too. Crying and talking. "All of it's in his bones. It's the actual stuff of his body and brain. The placenta you made from scratch. Your milk from nursing him. All those pancakes and school-lunch sandwiches, all of that food and care." She's looking into my face, nodding, even though I am fully winging it now, panicking, words pouring out like I'm a hose on the *weepy consolation* setting. "Everything you've ever fed him," I say. "His whole self is made completely out of your love."

The stream of words slows to a trickle and then stops. In the beat of silence, we hear the opening notes of *Fiddler*, Ruth clapping. Farrah Fawcett, Shapely's skittish, music-fearing golden retriever, darts into Edi's room to hide behind the door.

"Ash," Edi says. "Ash, my heart is breaking. I'm dying."

"I know," I say, and stop myself, in the nick of time, from saying, "Me too."

CHAPTER 4

Belle is sitting on the edge of the tub, watching me manage my acne with a look of unabashed horror on her perfect face. "Are you popping a pimple on your chin with the pin of an Obama badge? Mom," she says. "My god. I don't like to see that."

"So go, please. I feel like I have no memory of you knocking," I say. "But here you are!" Now I'm dabbing on a little medicated concealer.

"You could just get one of those pretend rocks that hides your keys," she says, "but, like, for your face."

"Thanks," I say.

"Mom," she says. "You're great, you're gorgeous, but seriously, what is *up* with your skin?"

"Stress?" I say. "Menopause? My badness pustuling out of me in pustules? I really have no idea." I dab balm on my lips. "Maybe I'm pregnant."

"Oh my god!" she says, looking up from her shin, where she's begun drawing a skull with a black eyeliner pencil. "Are you?"

"Please," I say. "I'm not. I'm kidding. My eggs are like a miserable old bunch of crone grapes."

"Yeah," Belle says. "Somebody already ate all the good ones. And now your body's like, *I guess this one's not too bad!* and picks the least wrinkled or moldy one to send down the chute."

"Thanks for elaborating," I say, but she's already interrupting, "But Mom! Mom! You could have a tiny little shrivelly raisin baby! We could keep it in a matchbox."

"Go. Get out of here," I say, swatting at her with a hand towel, but she doesn't move.

"Do you know that some people have something called a stone baby? It's actually super common. It's basically a baby that turns into a fossil before it's born. Wait. I'm looking it up." She taps on her phone. "Lithopedion. It's a calcified little baby. There have been as many as three hundred recorded cases in human history."

"I don't think I'd call that 'super common,'" I say.

"Wow, Mom. This woman had a stone baby at ninety! There's tons of time for you. Oh, here's a picture of one." She holds out her phone, and I lean over to look.

"Belle," I say. "That's a marble sculpture of god's hand with a sculpture of a baby in it." I look closer. "It's a garden ornament."

"So it is," she says. "But, ooooh, you can also buy a 3D-printed stone baby on eBay!" She shakes her head. "A plastic stone baby feels like a metaphor for something. Something that is definitely not good."

While it's true that I have birthed neither a raisin baby nor a stone baby, I did birth a not-quite baby when Belle was five. Honey and I hadn't wanted another baby, but as soon as I was pregnant, that fluffy little fact staggered to the edge of the nest and flew off. I hadn't wanted *a* baby, no, but I did want *this* baby. I felt taut and shiny with the secret of this tiny apple seed of a life. Honey was very "Whatever you want to do" about the pregnancy, which was technically the correct way to be, but also hurt my feelings. "Are you excited?" I'd ask, and he'd consider, say, "Excited? I mean . . ." and I'd say, "Forget it," and huff off to scramble an egg and then throw the whole pan, egg and all, into the trash because, suddenly, *eggs*. Ew.

But then there was blood in my underpants—not the familiar brownish smear, but bright horror-movie blood, lots of it, and I sobbed on my hands and knees on the bathroom floor while Honey sat on the closed toilet and quietly rubbed my back with one hand. I cramped out jellyfish clots—enormous and nearly black—and held them in my palms, yelling, "Don't come in!" when I heard the girls pattering around outside the door in their slippers. Honey looked abjectly terrified, like he'd seen a ghost, and that ghost was the ghost of his future marriage, when his warm and laughing wife would have turned into a weeping poltergeist, haunting him with her many obstetric *feelings*.

It wasn't his fault, of course. The thinnest thread of ambivalence does not yank a whole pregnancy into unraveling, I realize. But I was furious, I was lonely, and also, someone had slipped some kind of grief roofie into my cocktail, and it surged through my brain, obliterating both hope and reason. I wiped my face with my sleeve and pasted on a sunny smile whenever the girls crept into whichever room I was hiding out in. They would flip on the light and peer at me, fretful. I didn't want to try again. Even under the best of circumstances, a pregnancy feels like racing over uneven terrain with an egg in a spoon. So we didn't. We never did. We brought two kittens home from the shelter. I packed up my sorrow in an ugly box and hoped it would evaporate.

"Is Dad coming over?" Belle asks now, and I say, "Yeah," and she says, "Is that why you're putting on makeup?"

"It's tinted lip balm."

"But is that why?" she presses.

"I don't know," I say, and she says, "Fair," then asks, "Is Dad bringing food? Is it okay if Scriv comes over?"

"Yeah," I say. "Of course. I'd love that."

Scrivener is Belle's *theyfriend*. "Are you guys dating?" I'd said at some point, and she acted like I'd asked if they sat primly together on a Victorian fainting couch to read aloud from *The Bridges of Madison County* before exchanging locks of their hair. Or maybe she acted like I'd asked if they were *fucking*. It was honestly hard to tell which. "God!" she'd said. "No! Mom, ew. We're just hanging out."

"What does hanging out mean exactly?" I'd texted Jules and she'd texted back a smiley-face emoji and a cry-laughing emoji, which were not helpful.

"Do you want to maybe clean up the living room a little bit?" I say now, and this bit of nagging motivates Belle to, finally, stand up and leave the bathroom, calling back to me, "Nature abhors a vacuum cleaner."

By the time Belle and I get downstairs, Honey and Scriv are bursting into the house together, bringing with them the smell of spices and just a glimpse of the night outside, dark and wet, the sleet freezing into something that's less like snow than like heavier sleet. I push the door shut behind them while they're kicking off their boots.

Scriv is dressed like a Target employee—red polo shirt tucked into belted chinos—on account of working at Target. They dress more or less like this even when they're not working, though, and I can't tell if it's ironic or earnest or if there's even a difference. I'm an elderly mastodon, trying to understand the ways of the young humans, but Belle has explained that my need for clarity is part of the capitalist patriarchy's master plan, which I do not doubt for a second.

Honey hands me and Belle bags from India House, announcing their contents: "Samosas and pakoras. Saag paneer. Veggie korma. Makhani dal—I got a double order—and aloo chaat. Biryani. There should be some chutneys in there. And some naan."

"Yum," I keep saying. "This looks so good. Thank you."

Everything's on the table, the candles lit against the darkness, fragrant food in abundance. "Humor me," I say. "Can we just take a moment to think of Edi, send her our love?" And I know it's bad because Belle doesn't even mock me or apologize to Scriv or announce that the hypocritical half-Jews are saying grace. She just says, "Of course, Mom." I squinch my eyes shut like a child, picture Edi's face. Then I picture peeling pink hearts from a sheet of stickers, pressing them onto Edi's cheeks. Is this what praying is? I honestly have no idea.

We eat. We eat and eat! We pass containers around the table, spoon out heaps of rice and curries, exclaim over heat and deliciousness, swipe fried things through sauces, guess at spice combinations. I can't stop thanking Honey, and he keeps saying, "Please. Ash, stop. It's really my pleasure." At some point he kneels in front of the woodstove to add a log, and the sight of his broad, helpful shoulders fills me with regret.

I have a memory, suddenly, of Honey serving us a beautiful lamb stew years ago, before the girls were both vegetarians. There were white beans in it, cinnamon, and the kids kept saying, "Delicious!" with gravy on their chins. Honey's eyes had been shining with happiness. "I rolled all the couscous from scratch and cooked it in a special steamer." He beamed. I'd put my fork down, stopped chewing. "Honey, we're so busy—we don't even have time to, like, *floss*—and couscous is so easy. You can't just make it from the box?" "I don't know," he'd said, and then added, terribly, "I'm sorry." "No, no," I'd said quickly. "I'm sorry to be ungrateful. Thank you for this." But sometimes I worried that marriage was just a series of these small deflations, our dreams floating around invisibly near the ceiling like escaped gas.

Now Belle brings a box of rose-scented Turkish delight to the table. "Press kit?" Honey says, and I nod. I write about food, so I get tons

33

of weird, unsolicited stuff in the mail: an entire crate of pineapple cottage cheese; two dozen packages of seaweed jerky; a single bag of brisket-flavored popcorn; a fleece blanket screen-printed with a lurid photograph of lasagna. A mysterious box arriving is pretty much our favorite thing, and I always wait to open it until Belle gets home from school. "It's . . . canned cuttlefish cutlets? God. Did Dr. Seuss send us this?" Even the bad stuff is fun.

Scriv has nibbled the edge of a sugar-dusted square. "Sweet, gelatinous bubble bath," they say, which is accurate.

"Turkish *delight*," Belle says. "It's so presumptuous. I feel like, hey, we'll decide if we're delighted or not."

"Truth," Scriv says.

I am smiling and smiling. Belle looks at me. "Mom," she says. "You love us all so much! We know. You're so glad we're here. Please don't say it."

"I wasn't going to!" I lie, cryingly, and she shakes her head, laughs, and pats my shoulder.

"Thumper, get down," Honey scolds, but he's kidding. The cats aren't allowed on the table, which would be meaningful only if anybody communicated this to them. Instead, Thumper strolls over and head-butts Honey, languidly licks his plate, then flops over onto his back, knocking over the saltshaker and an empty water glass. "Bad, bad cattie," Honey says, and scoops him up. "You get a million kisses of punishment."

I do like a man who likes a cat.

But now you're thinking Honey's perfect and why aren't we together and probably it's my fault, and you're right about all of it, more or less. If I were going to summarize it, I'd tell you that I can't be with a person who, in the middle of the worst fight ever, leaves me weeping in the bed to take a shower, where I hear him joyfully singing "No

Woman, No Cry." "Were you *singing in the shower?*" I'd said when he came cheerfully back into the room with a Q-tip in each ear, and he'd scrunched up his nose, said, "Oof. Was I?" "Do you have any actual human feelings?" I'd asked, and he hadn't answered, sensibly, because it was a trick question. "What do you want from me, Ash?" he asked, and I said, "More."

I did. I wanted more.

Belle has made a pot of chai and brought more random freebies to the table: pretzels filled with Nutella, gluten-free macarons in a rainbow of sherbet flavors, and something that identifies itself as a Chocolate Superfoods Bar, "Now with more açaí!" "This right here is my kind of party," I say, and pour Honey and me each another glass of wine. Only then my phone rings, which means either my parents or Shapely, and everyone freezes while I look. It's the hospice.

"Ash?" It's Violet, one of the nurses. "Hey. Sorry. But you should probably come over."

CHAPTER 5

Violet finds me breathless from sprinting over the frozen parking lot, crying and rubbing my hands together at the sanitizing station. "It's okay," she says. "I'm sorry to scare you. She's just having a bad night." I tell her I'm glad she called, follow her to Edi's room.

Edi is curled onto her side, bloated and pale, sobbing. "Ash," she says. "Ash, I'm so thirsty."

I sit on the edge of her bed. "I know you are, sweetheart," I say. "Let's get you something to drink."

"But my nightgown is wet," she says. I peel back the covers. Her PEG tube is leaking and everything is soaked with bile and soda and whatever Edi ate for dinner. Risotto? In the big picture: Edi is dying. In the small picture: This is so gross. Both things.

"Here," Violet says gently, tugging the blankets aside, and Edi says, "Can you just let Ash?" I try not to telepath my desperation— *Don't leave me!*—and I must succeed, because Violet says, "Of course," slips out, and pulls the door closed behind her.

You know when you put on a sweater in the car, and then when you get to where you're going you can't figure out how to get out of your seat belt? That's what it's like trying to peel Edi out of her clothes.

There are so many tubes and wires, and each article of clothing has to be threaded carefully over everything, like you're untangling a necklace, only with fluids involved, and also veins. The nurses make it look easy, but by the time I'm done, Edi's nightgown is somehow scrunched around the base of the IV pole and she's shivering.

I grab her a blanket from the warmer, and she huddles under it while I open dresser drawers. "This?" I say, holding up something ruffly and flannel, and she shakes her head. Not the next one either, which is *ugh, too stripey.* "You're very picky," I say, and she smiles.

"The one from Jules," she says. It's a black long-sleeved T-shirt that my daughter has silk-screened with the brief Helvetica list FUCK & CANCER & FUCK. The rethreading commences, and by the time Edi's propped back up against the pillows, her PEG tube has leaked again. A wet spot is spreading across her front. "Are you fucking kidding me?" she says, and then, "Ugh, Ash. Just fucking leave it. I can't even. Grab me a towel, okay?" She stuffs it under her shirt, lies back, and closes her eyes.

"I'm literally dying of thirst," she says. (She literally is.) "Can you get me a Dr Pepper? And also the rest of that watermelon juice? Honey brought it. It's in a fancy bottle in the communal fridge." I retrieve the drinks, grab fresh straws, fill an ice bucket, refill the water pitcher, say hi to Junior's niece, who is also rooting around the various refrigerators. Everything is hushed save the hum of the dryer and the nurses laughing quietly at their station, Ruth singing to herself behind her closed door. Shapely feels like a regular house in some ways—the kitchen, say, which is just a messy, normal kitchen, with clipped bags of chips and scolding notes on the fridge (LABEL YOUR LEFTOVERS!) or the regular detergent-scented laundry room with its fabric softener sheets and plastic baskets, its piles of towels and gigantic underpants. In other ways—like the nurses' station, the wall-mounted hand sanitizers, the mechanical beds—it feels like a hospital.

But in most ways what it feels like is a haunted B and B: lots of silk-flower décor and peeling, patterned wallpaper; many porcelain figurines of whistling white children carrying buckets and baskets; plenty of cross-stitched wit and inspiration, like ALL GUESTS MUST BE APPROVED BY THE DOG and LET ME LIVE IN THE HOUSE BY THE SIDE OF THE ROAD AND BE A FRIEND TO MAN. (*What?*) "It's very homey here," they told Edi at the intake, and she said, "It really is," and winked at me like the snob she is.

Back in her room, Edi drinks and drinks while I drop clothes in her laundry hamper and refold the clean nighties. "Ahh," she says finally. "There's nothing like drinking to quench your thirst," and I say, "That is the truth."

I drag a chair by the windowsill, pull up the trash can, and spread a towel in my lap. "Bouquet duty?" Edi says. "Those flowers aren't going to tidy up themselves." It's silly, I know, but I love doing it: turning five or six bedraggled vases of flowers into a couple of perfect ones. I cull out everything dead, trim off slimy or curling leaves, rearrange what's left by color and size, rinse out the vases, and refill them with fresh water. If you're ever sending anyone flowers, you should know that carnations and mums last forever. Lilacs and irises are basically dead by the time they arrive. Roses can go either way. Hydrangeas go quickly, but on the sly—they still look pretty, even after they're dry as paper.

"Look at this," Edi says, and I look. She's got her shirt hoisted up, and I lean over to check her PEG tube insertion.

"It looks okay," I say, and she says, "No, no. Look at this scar." She traces a finger below her belly button, where the skin is puckered and mauve.

"It's beautiful," I say, before launching into a mini-inspirational lecture on brokenness and how the light gets in, which segues into my poignant thoughts on *kintsugi*, the Japanese art of mending cracked pottery with gold. "In the end there's more beauty in the imperfection," I conclude rousingly. (Oh my god, *why?*)

Edi is staring at me in openmouthed horror. "Well," she says, finally. "That's all very *wabi-sabi* and wonderful. But I feel like I'm pretty much mended with shit and that's how the shit gets in and stop, okay?"

"Okay," I say, and lean all the way over to kiss her irritated face. "Sorry." She pats my cheek forgivingly.

"And anyways, I was just trying to show you the way that one scar intersects with my C-section scar from Dash. It's, like, a whole situation down there."

"I know," I say, and then I open my mouth to say something else—who even knows what—and she waves her arm to shush me. I understand. What can I say about this topographical mapping of birth and death? Everything is right there. Right here.

A text dings in. "Hi Ash," it says, and I type, "Hi Dash!"

"Hows mom"

"She's good," I type back. "She's right here. Do you want to talk to her?"

"Na goodnight"

"Sleep tight!" I text back.

"Texting one of your boyfriends?" Edi asks, and I say, "Ha ha, very funny. Just work stuff." I don't like to lie, but do sometimes anyway. Edi's got a glass in each hand, sipping from one straw and then the other. She refuses to drink out of plastic because it maybe gives you cancer, which makes me cringe all the way to the marrow of my bones, where my own cancers are probably replicating even as I reflect on Edi's ironic convictions.

"How's your falling-in-love disorder going?" she asks, and I move my hand side to side, say, "Eh." She nods. "I'm a little in love with

Junior, to be honest," I say, and she says, "Of course you are. Maybe don't get too attached to Junior."

"Hey," I say. "I'm an optimist."

"Ash," she says. "You drive with your hazards on *for no reason*. You are not an optimist."

I shrug, prick my finger, pop it in my mouth, taste blood. A thorn! On a rose! It's like a fairy tale, like a metaphor, but also it's just my messy, foolish, painful life. The wind rattles the windows, whips rain against them, and I throw an extra blanket over Edi's legs, finish up the flowers.

As adults, Edi and I have had a very city-mouse/country-mouse kind of friendship. She can't understand how I can bear to live anywhere but New York, but then she loves to visit us here and twirl through the farmers' market—"Not the same as *Cumberland* Farms," she realized belatedly after a disappointing stop there—where she buys shit-speckled eggs and gleaming local honey, cartons of tiny wild blueberries, rubber-banded bouquets of stinking wild ramps, and shrink-wrapped packages of pasture-fed lamb loin, which she schleps back to Brooklyn in a cooler. We've taken her to many strangely dull festivals—Onions and Art, Sheep and Shawls, Septoberfest—where there was nothing to do but eat charred, overpriced kabobs, look languidly at handmade pottery spoon rests, and watch the kids watch the men and women who were spinning yarn, grinding corn, peeling apple after apple. We took her to pick strawberries once too, and she said to the old, overalled farmer, "How do you stop people from picking in the night and not paying?" He scratched his straw-hatted head like he'd come straight from central casting, and said thoughtfully, "Well, now, I guess we don't. I guess if someone needs to come and pick in the night, then that's all right. We can spare some berries."

"Schooled by the berry guy!" I said to Edi in the car, and she said, "Seriously."

Sometimes I think Edi pictures something more E. M. Forster than what I have to offer. "Should we picnic by the sea?" she once asked dreamily, and I had to be like, "Um, Edi. We're two hours from the *sea*. We can picnic by the patchouli-scented youth on the town common." But, then, when I visit her, all I want to do is order in because oh my god, what you can have delivered in Brooklyn! You can call for your mussels and frites, and then, while you're hanging up the phone, they're already arriving, the French fries still so hot you have to blow on them. "Should we make spaghetti?" Edi would always ask, and I'd be like, "No. We should order fried chicken from the Korean place and also tiramisu from the tiramisu place."

It was tricky with my parents, that I wanted to stay over at Edi's sometimes when we were visiting. But I had to explain how much I longed for that time with her and Jude after the girls would go to bed finally, and Honey and I could loll around on their California king, drinking chianti out of ceramic cups, eating bags of fancy Park Slope cheese puffs, and making each other laugh until we cried. Jude played us voice-mail recordings of his great-aunt: "Jude? Jude? Is this your phone or is this the other phone?" Then you'd hear her say to her ancient husband, "Irv, I think this is the other phone."

Edi and I shared stories with Jude and Honey from before we knew them, like the time in second grade when Edi's family took me on a cruise with them, and Edi and Jonah's dad sat on a deck chair, reading *Shogun*, in a row of at least five other dads reading *Shogun* in deck chairs. We'd open another bottle of wine. We'd imitate the girls from earlier in the day: Jules, six, trying to learn how to swing her arms when she walked, and looking more and more like a self-conscious chimpanzee. Or grouchy three-year-old Belle, at the Central Park Zoo, pointing at everything with her angry thumb: "I don't *yike* my sandals! I don't *yike* those penguins! I don't *yike* you yaffing at me!"

Eventually, it got harder. Edi and Jude were trying to get pregnant and were not getting pregnant. Reinforcements were summoned in the form of drugs, of intrauterine insemination, of scrubbed sperm and burning shots in the ass. One round of IVF produced a faint trace of a pregnancy that didn't stick, like a Post-it note fluttering to the floor from a wall calendar. Edi wanted to see me, but not the girls, which was fair, though Jules and Belle were sad. "But *tell* her we're sad," Belle said crankily once, as I was leaving for New York, and I said, "I might not tell her that? But I really, really know you're sad." On a spring day in Prospect Park, every single woman was hugely, ripely pregnant, splitting open at the seams, spilling out of her silk jersey maternity tunic. It was no better up by us, where Edi pointed once in town and said, "I'm sorry, but are *both* of those pregnant women wearing cutoff hemp overalls?" (They were.)

And then, finally, there was an embryo that would be Dash, and, although there were various implantation scares and fluctuating hormone levels and the time Edi was convinced she had barfed him out into a city trash can, he would not be dislodged. After his birth, the girls took turns holding him. They were older by then—twelve and nine—and they bottle-fed him and changed his diaper, musing in hushed voices over the similarities and differences between him and their old Baby Alive, including the fact that the plastic doll had neither a black and suppurating belly-button stub nor a scabby and terrifying circumcision wound. "But both their heads smell powdery and good," Jules concluded. Edi, exhausted, leaned her head on my shoulder and cried. "I can't believe I prayed for this," she said, and I said, "First of all, you can totally believe it. And second of all, you don't pray."

"True," she said. "But I *would have* prayed for this."

"And your prayers would have been answered," I said. "Except about the part where your vag got all tattered apart." And I stood to retrieve her donut gel cushion from the freezer.

"Hey." It's Dr. Soprano now, sticking his head in the door and whispering. Edi is asleep again, surrounded by empty cans and bottles and cups like a cartoon drunk. "Ash, do you have a minute?" His handsome face is unsmiling. "Of course," I say. "Give me one second." I shake the towel out over the trash can and move the newly empty vases to a shelf over the dresser.

I follow him out into the hallway and then into the laundry room. He pushes the door closed behind me. "I was hoping to talk to you," he says.

"I think I know what this is about," I say. I can feel my heart beating, jangling under my ribs.

Dr. Soprano presses my shoulders back against the door, pushes his thigh between my legs. "Is it about how slutty I am?" I say, and he says, "Shhh, yes," brushes his lips against my neck, grabs my hair in his fist the way he knows I like. I am weak in the knees. But actually. Something is maybe wrong with the muscles in my legs. (Parkinson's?) I slide to the floor, and he presses the lock in the doorknob, lifts me, places me gently on top of the dryer, which tumbles beneath me. There are plastic baskets everywhere, filled with bibs and blankets and waterproof lap pads, all the linens of everybody's last days, everything smelling of Dreft and Bounce. We hear *Fiddler* starting deep in the house, Farrah Fawcett scrabbling to come in. I just want this. Not even the sex exactly, but the being wanted. The oblivion of it. Someone else's feelings crowding mine out, burning them clean. "But I'm so tired," I say from the warm, humming metal of the dryer, and Dr. Soprano, kneeling on the floor to unbutton my jeans, says, "Shhh, Ash. You don't have to do a thing."

CHAPTER 6

"Pretend you're dead," Edi says to me, and I collapse in my chair with my tongue lolling out. Edi laughs and scores it a six. We've been playing this game since we were little, and it's always cracked us up. "Is it still funny in hospice, though?" she says now, and I say, "Definitely."

"You're writing?" she says, pointing to my laptop. I shrug.

"Not really," I say. "I don't know. I'm just making some notes. I didn't actually realize you were awake."

"Notes about Shapely?" she asks, and I shrug again.

"Yeah, I guess. I don't know."

"Hospice makes for pretty good copy," she says. She's poking at a cold grilled cheese sandwich by her bed. "But there's not a ton of suspense. I mean, the narrative arc is kind of predictable."

"If you know what I mean," she adds to make me laugh, and I laugh.

I point to her uneaten sandwich and ask if she wants something else—soup or an egg or some pudding.

"Sicilian lemon polenta pound cake," she says. "Seriously. That's what I want."

Sicilian lemon polenta pound cake is Edi's holy grail. She bought a piece at Dean & DeLuca in the mid-1990s, claimed it was the best cake she'd ever eaten, and then could never find it again. Even the very next week, when she returned to the store, they didn't know what she was talking about and had no record of such a cake in their inventory. "It's like a ghost ship," she said. "But cake." Over the years she has tried lots of recipes for similar-sounding cakes, but nothing has ever really come close. Did it have rosemary? Olive oil? Were they Meyer lemons or regular? She has never been sure, and has only gotten less sure as the decades pass. "Did you maybe just *imagine* the cake?" I asked her once, and she shook her head. "I ate it in real life," she said dreamily. "The best cake."

We're compiling a little cookbook for Dash—all of his favorites that she's always made for him—and Edi has tasked me with including a recipe for The Cake. "Edi, we don't *have* a recipe for The Cake," I've reminded her. "That's the whole problem." She has reassured me, maddeningly, that it's a problem I'm sure to solve.

"I think one of the volunteers made lemon-poppy-seed muffins," I say now, and she rolls her eyes.

"There should be Make-a-Wish for grown-ups," she says. "And I could ask for the recipe for that cake, and, like, Lady Gaga would bake it for me. I just want to taste it one more time." She sighs. "I think someone made mushroom-barley soup," she says, defeated. "Maybe that?"

Edi and I have always loved to eat together. In elementary school, we were the only kids who liked hot lunch—or, at least, the only kids who admitted to liking it. And we liked all of it, with all of its made-up imperialist names. We liked the salty chicken chow mein, which they served in a gloppy pile topped with crunchy noodles from a can. We liked the similarly salty chicken à la king, studded with celery and peas, though it was hard to picture royalty eating it. We liked the oily Spanish rice and the unpopular fish sticks, the even less popular fish *cakes*, and also the cakey squares of pizza they served on Fridays. We liked the sloppy joes and the oddly shaggy hamburgers, the mild macaroni and cheese and the "*American* chop suey," as if there were any other kind. Also, we liked the little dishes of pudding and Jell-O and still do, which is good, because there's tons of it here at Shapely.

Farrah Fawcett clacks into the kitchen while I'm heating soup in the microwave. She sits in front of me, gazing soulfully into my face, and I can practically see the thought bubble over her head with a picture of cheese in it. "One tiny piece," I whisper to her, and grab a block of American slices out of the fridge. "Don't tell the others." But somebody's corgi runs in at the sound of the wrapper. "I don't even know you," I say to it. "And you're much too short for cheese." It knits its fuzzy little brow. "Okay," I whisper, "one *tiny* piece for you too."

"That's Mr. Pinky Pie," Violet says, on her way in with a tray of empty sippy cups. "He came with the new folks in room four. Wait, Ash, are you still here from before?"

"Wow," I say. "I don't know." I remember Honey waking in the night once when I was hunched over the newborn Jules, asking blearily, "Are you *still* nursing her or are you nursing her *again*?" It was such an exhausting existential question that I'd burst into tears.

"I guess I'm still here?" I laugh. "I mean, I didn't end up going home, so yeah." I hear myself sounding more casual than I actually felt in the night in the cot in Edi's room with my head on a Shapely pillow. *Someone probably died with their head on this very pillow!* I'd thought to myself, like an asshole, and shuddered, both about the dead head and also about being an asshole. In a cartoon, you would have just seen my petrified eyeballs in the dark room. Also, I thought I could hear somebody barfing, which further petrified me because I have an actually diagnosable fear of the sound of barfing. I'd pressed the scary corpse pillow around my ears and been too afraid to move.

"Are you awake?" I'd texted Belle a little later in the night, wishing I were home with her, and she'd written back immediately, "Yeah dad's here everything okay?" "Totally! Everything's good! Good-night, Sweetie," I'd texted, and she'd written, "Jelly and Thumper say hi & Dad says hi too."

"What about you?" I say to Violet now. "Are you still here or back?"

"Still here," she says, "but I'm leaving as soon as I eat all of the brownies. Hey, don't give Pinky Pie too much cheese. I heard he's got gas. And you can leave that cot made up in Edi's room. We don't need it anywhere else right now."

"Thanks," I say, then, "Wait, is his name just Pinky Pie or is it *Mr.* Pinky Pie?"

"Just Pinky Pie," Violet says.

The soup dings and I take it out, stir it. "Enjoy your afternoon," I say, and she says, "You too. Take care, Ash. I'll make sure the new shift checks on you guys."

There are people in the hallway outside Edi's room, and she's confused when I get back. "They brought a crib into the room across the hall," she says. "That's so weird. Why would you bring your baby to hospice with you? They couldn't get someone to care for it at home?"

"I don't know," I say. But when I peek across, I see an IV pole by the crib, a woman with her face crumpled like a paper bag full of sorrow, the baby in her arms. I must make a sound because Edi says, "What?"

"Nothing," I say. "I don't know."

A text dings in from Belle about milk and are we out of it. "If there isn't any, then yeah," I write back. *Kids!* "Why aren't you at school?" I text, and three dots appear, then nothing.

"Should I worry about Belle skipping so much school?" I say to Edi, and she shrugs. "She seems okay to me," she says. She blows on a spoonful of soup. "But I know teenagers are not always as they seem."

Edi and I grew up together in New York, and once, in tenth grade, walking the five blocks that separated our apartments, we stopped half a dozen times to vomit up vast, clear pools of the vodka we'd stolen from her parents' pantry. Probably we were dressed like Madonna in *Desperately Seeking Susan*, so our hair was held conveniently back for us by knotted headscarves. I told my parents we had a stomach virus. "Both of you?" my dad asked from the doorway of the bathroom, where Edi was lying groaningly in the empty tub and I had my cheek pressed to the cool tiles of the floor. "Yup," I said. "What are the chances?" he said mildly, and then left us to it. Weirdly, though, I think this was probably an example of teenagers being *exactly* what they seem.

"Her dad is a bougie drug dealer," I say now. "Plus, nobody's exactly accusing me of being a helicopter parent right now, if you know what I mean."

"I'm sorry, Ash," Edi says, and grimaces, and I say, "Oh god, no. I didn't mean because of you. I just meant. I don't know. I'm just kind of preoccupied with work and stuff." *Stuff like you dying*, I don't say. *Stuff like schtupping your brother. Among other people.*

Edi is shaking the PEG tube like it's a ballpoint pen that won't write. There's a stuck mushroom, and we watch as the liquid builds up behind it then dislodges it with a tiny whoosh. "Phew," she says as the bag fills with soup.

When we were teenagers, dabbling amateurishly in various eating disorders, we had actually wished for this exact thing. "If only you could eat and eat but it would all go into, like, a plastic bag instead of your stomach!" I swear—Edi literally said that once. I remind myself for the zillionth time not to recall this aloud.

"It's like Mr. Thirsty," I say instead, about the spit-sucking machine at the dentist we both went to as kids.

"Oh my god! It's exactly like Mr. Thirsty!" Edi says. "But, like, if he were really *really* thirsty, like, punishingly thirsty, and ended up sucking out all your stomach contents."

"Do you think Dr. Zolgati molested you?" I ask, even though I already know the answer. Our dentist was kind of famously accused of sexually abusing kids who were under sedation, and then he kind of famously shot himself in the head, which did not overly reassure our parents that the accusations had been false.

"I still think no?" Edi says. "But also? Besides that it seems like it was mostly boys, I don't really care that much. I mean, I was, like, gassed and laughing my head off or whatever, getting my teeth drilled apart while he—what? Stuck his hand in my Minnie Mouse shorts? It kind of gives me a *tree falls nobody hears it* feeling."

"Same," I say.

"Why do you look like that?" she says. "What?"

"Nothing," I say. What I look like is probably like a crazy smiling person. "I mean. I don't know. I just love you so much."

Edi rolls her eyes. "Because of how I feel about being maybe groped by the same dentist as you?" she says, and I say, "I guess, yeah."

"I love you too," she says.

We hear Ruth clapping, *Fiddler* starting, Farrah Fawcett scrabbling down the hallway followed by Pinky Pie. The music blares on, and then the baby is crying, the mom yelling, "Can somebody please turn that down?" the baby crying louder and louder, inconsolable.

"Oh, Ash," Edi says, inhaling sharply. "It's *the baby*."

And I say, "I don't know. Yeah. I think it might actually be the baby."

"Oh, Ash," Edi says again. The baby is screaming, and Pinky Pie scrambles into my lap, shivering, and a terrible doggy cheese-fart smell fills the room. "I know," I say, waving a hand in front of my face and also crying. "It is not actually bearable."

CHAPTER 7

"Why are you so noisy?" Belle is chastising Thumper, who is lying on her chest, purring into her face. "You're too noisy. Where's your brother?" She calls Jelly, who jumps up and crowds onto her. Thumper sighs like a beleaguered person, stands indignantly, and staggers over to flop down into my puddle of boobs. "You're so bony," Belle complains to Jelly. "You better not be getting old or you'll be in big trouble." She grabs his cheeks and kisses him all over his whiskery face.

We're lying in my bed, which is where we mostly are these days when we're home together, just the two of us. We've taken to eating in here, even, which seems like a dangerous trend, a slippery slope that's slip-sliding us into a dumpster future filled with garbage and rats, but I don't seem to have the energy to fight it. Tonight we got a pizza and brought it straight to bed. Now Belle lifts a half-eaten olive slice over the cat and bites into it.

"Bellini," I say. "Do you want to talk about school and why you're skipping so much of it?"

Belle shakes her head, chews, swallows, kisses Jelly's snout, says, "Not really. And it's not even that much of it. Just some." A tiny garnet winks from the side of her nose. Her face! I have never not had the impulse, inaugurated by her birth, to bite her ripe, plummy cheeks. It only gets worse as my own face dries up. The existence of prunes should always have been a cautionary tale about aging.

"Okay," I say.

She looks at me, narrows her eyes suspiciously. "Don't bite my face," she says, and I say, "I'll try not to."

"Do you love Jules more than me because she's less weird?" Belle asks out of nowhere. "I would totally understand if you did. I mean, I pretty much do." This kid.

"I do not," I say. "I love you both the same exact amounts of infinity. Even though it's true she may be somewhat less weird than you are. But there's something almost weird about how not weird she is." I'm thinking of the normal niece on *The Munsters*—a reference Belle wouldn't know—but if the normal niece were, you know, a brilliant engineering student.

"True!" Belle says, delighted.

A text dings in from Edi: "Come take me outside?"

"It's freezing!" I text back, and she texts, "I don't care."

"Okay," I write. "Be there in 10."

Belle is reading over my shoulder. "Come to Shapely with me?" I say, and she says, "Yeah. I'm driving, though."

Inside the hospice, Belle glows like a shiny ambassador from the land of youth. It feels almost indecent to bring her. "Belle!" Edi cries when she sees her. "Oh, yay!"

"Hi," Belle says, and leans over to kiss Edi's cheek, a little shy. Hospice is just so existentially weird. It's like you walk in under a giant banner that says, EVERYONE HERE IS DYING! but then most of the time you're just making small talk and quesadillas, trying to find something to watch on Netflix, or wondering if there's any pie left. "I mean, isn't that just life, though?" Jonah had said to me when I described this. "We're doing all the things, enjoying ourselves where we can, even though we're all just going to die at the end of it?" "Geez, Jonah," I'd said. "Too much fucking perspective?" he asked, because all the men in my life like to quote from *Spinal Tap* whenever the occasion arises. But yes. Too much fucking perspective.

Violet comes in while we're bundling Edi up, smiles at us. "Are they breaking you out?" she says to Edi, and Edi says, "Yup. Finally!"

Violet helps us sort out the tubes and wires, the down jacket and blankets and slippers, helps us help Edi from the edge of the bed into the wheelchair, which is inexplicably more epic than it sounds—like trying to get your suitcase into the overhead bin, only it's made of heavy, floppy bones and cries out sometimes. Edi grimaces every few seconds, and it's terrible. "Eds," I say, grimacing myself, and she says, "No, no. I'm good."

"To life, to life, *l'chaim*!" Belle is singing along, then stops, peering into the hallway. "Is that a *crib*?" she whispers, and I nod. She raises her eyebrows questioningly, and I shake my head, shrug. "Oof," she says.

"Are you guys just going into the courtyard?" Violet asks. "Would you be willing to take Farrah out to pee?" Violet inherited Farrah Fawcett from a longtime resident of the hospice who died last year. There's an elderly Chihuahua floating around here too, adopted by Violet in a similar fashion, but he's usually cowering under the desk at the nurses' station.

"Of course," I say. "Do you want us to take Tiny too?"

"Nah," she says. "He's scared of the courtyard. Here, let's finish getting everybody ready."

The sun rises and sets, rises and sets, calendar pages fly off the wall, the roses bud, open, wilt, drop all their petals, the ice caps finish melting, the seas rise, and finally Edi is ready to go. "I kind of have to pee," she says, and I laugh, say, "Okay."

I remember a long-ago snow day. Jules insisted on dressing herself, so I left her to it while I changed Belle's diaper, noodled her fat little arms and kicky little legs into wooly long underwear, stuffed her whole round wooly little self into a down sack, and zipped it up carefully over her tummy and under her many chins. When I looked up again, Jules had stuffed both feet down one leg of her snowsuit and also zipped her hair into it. She cried and cried while I gentled her hair out of the zipper and tugged out her legs. "Don't help me!" She was sobbing and furious, and then finally—rocked in my arms, face patted dry with a tissue—consoled. Had the snow already melted by now? I peered out the window. It had not! Jules stood up from my lap to pull on her boots, and then Belle, from the carpet, where she was still on her back waving her little arms and legs around like an upended tortoise, announced proudly, "Mama, I pooping!"

Violet, paged away by another patient, calls back to me, "Get her to go in the hat, okay?" The hat is a kind of bucket in the toilet that measures something about the volume of urine or maybe its composition. But after we successfully navigate the wheelchair and the bathroom and the IV pole and the leggings, the fact of the hat makes Edi unable to pee. "Sorry," she says. "I'm having performance anxiety. Hang on."

"Please," I say. "Edi. Take your time. We're not in a massive rush to get home and lie around depressively."

Belle is sitting in a chair, chuckling into her phone and eating Edi's candy, and her easy presence is such a bright spot that I have to express my love or I'll die. (Not actually, though!) So I say, "Careful. Some of that's stuff Dad brought over."

"Yoiks!" she says, then looks at the package. "I think these are just regular non-weed jelly beans."

"They are," Edi confirms.

"Can I eat some of this trail mix, Edi?" Belle calls in, and Edi says, "Of course."

"Ugh," Belle says. "If there's anything more depressing than a sun-dried nectarine, I couldn't tell you what it is." I catch her eye and she grimaces, because, I'm guessing, *hospice*, but Edi just says, "Seriously," then pees a little, shrugs.

"All this for *that*?" I say, and she laughs.

And then we're wheeling her through the hallway, Belle pushing the pole, Farrah click-clacking along excitedly, all of us bursting out into the frozen night like triumph itself.

"Oh!" Edi cries. "Oh my god." The whole domed black sky is above us, punctured with its infinite glittering star holes. It is breathtaking. Or we're just breathless because of the cold. Probably both. "Oh my god," Edi says again. "It's the *ceilings* inside that were the problem!" She's smiling and smiling, crying a little bit, and I catch myself committing her face to memory—and then guiltily erasing it. And then, panicked, committing it to memory again.

Farrah squats and pees, lifts up one paw and then another. "I think her feet are cold," Belle says.

"No, no," Edi says. "Don't take me back in. Oh my god, you guys. Take me home with you! Kidnap me. Please." I must look stricken, because she says, quickly, "I'm kidding. This is good. This is exactly what I needed. Just give me another minute."

She's shivering, though, and I squat down to wrap my arms around her from behind the chair, and Belle leans down to wrap her arms around me, and I think we must look like a page from a picture book. *The Wrap-Arounds*, it would be called, with the dog stepping on our feet and grinning because she's in on the joke, whatever it is.

"Okay," Edi announces through her chattering teeth. "I'm good."

And then we're back inside with a whoosh, Shapely warm and bustling and bright, scented with freshly baked oatmeal cookies, filled with the music of resilience and optimism, all of it heartbreaking, all of it terrible.

"Wonder of wonders," Edi and Belle are singing along. "Miracle of miracles!"

Of course. It's these things too.

CHAPTER 8

Because it's the middle of a school day, I'm surprised when my door opens and Belle flies into the room. "Oh my god, Mom!" she says. "Lock your fucking door! Wait. Is that a *woman*?" She looks, nods approvingly. "Okay, okay. Solid." She leans in to fist-bump me, peers closer. "Miss Norman?"

"Hey, Belle."

"Oh, shit," I say.

"Mom," Belle says. "You have to sleep with my eighth-grade gym teacher like you're in a play about someone's bisexual mom?"

"I really only ever *subbed* in the middle school," Miss Norman says, somewhat irrelevantly.

"I thought you coached women's crew at the college," I say and she nods, says, "I do."

"Miss Norman—Jen—volunteers at Shapely," I say. "That's how we know each other."

"Not super interested, tbh," Belle says, scrunching up her nose. "I mean, I actually *am* kind of interested? But also I think maybe I'll just talk to you later." She scoops Jelly off the dresser and closes the door behind her as she leaves.

"Fuck," I say, and Jen says, "I'm so sorry."

"No, no," I say. "Totally not your fault. Plus, I'll get partial credit for you being a woman. *Miss Norman*."

Miss Norman laughs. "I hope I made it worth your while, at least," she says smugly, probably remembering her own formidable expertise and the sound of me crying out like a cartoon character falling from a crumbling bridge into an echoing canyon, and I smile, say, "You did." I don't say anything else for fear that I'll mention how grindingly tired I am, how I actually just craved the desire, the before part, everybody wet and wanting, and then I wanted to climb out of bed and put my pajamas on—pull on the flannel bottoms and button the top all the way up—and curl against her quietly and go to sleep. I am not under the impression that this information would be welcome.

I wonder for the millionth time what is wrong with me. When I was eleven or twelve, my friend Paul's mom was in graduate school for psychology, and she'd asked my parents if she could use me for her dissertation research. In her dark-walled office, beneath a brass desk lamp, she showed me ink blots, and explained the idea—that I should just tell her what I saw, without censoring myself or worrying what she would think. Anything was completely fine! And what I saw was an old woman getting reamed by a horse. I saw a massive erection sandwiched between somebody's pimply butt cheeks. Oh, and this one was something dripping from a lady's vagina hole! I'm sure I didn't even have the language for what I was seeing—but I didn't need it, because I wouldn't have spoken any of it anyway. "A dragonfly?" I said out loud instead, vaguely, gesturing at one mirrored image. "Someone playing a harpsichord?" I said about another. She nodded and smiled, convinced of my innocence.

Decades later I was with Paul in a bar, confessing to him over Manhattans how his mom had inadvertently proven to me that I was a middle-school criminal pervert. His mother was long dead at the time, and he laughed out loud. "Oh, she became famous for that experiment!" he said. "She'd had pornographic photographs turned into those Rorschach-type images. It wasn't you. They were all just actually filthy pictures. Her research was about sex and shame." Somehow, at the time, this felt like a metaphor for my entire relationship to myself.

"I should probably go home and walk my dogs," Miss Norman says now. "As soon as I'm done watching you put your hair up in that ponytail. Girls and their hair." She whistles.

"Butches and girls and their hair," I say, and she laughs. I finish twisting the rubber band. "Yeah. I should probably . . ." I shake my head, shrug. "Do something or other." She laughs again, dresses herself in her gray sweatpants and gray hoodie, kisses my cheek. "Call me?" I say, and she says, "Of course. Take care of yourself, Ash," and leaves.

"Are you still here or are you back at school?" I text Belle. "Also, sorry about the whole Miss Norman thing! Ack!" How my life turned into an endless episode of *Three's Company* is a complete mystery to me.

I text Jonah and Jude a brief Edi update about her evolving electrolyte situation. "New restaurant idea," Jonah texts back. "Magnesium! The menu is okra and mackerel and chard." "Yum," I text.

I text Honey, "Any luck with The Cake?" He knows someone who knows someone who maybe worked at Dean & DeLuca in the 1990s. He's promised to pursue it. "A tiny lead," he texts back right away. "I'll tell you when I see you."

"Magnesium!" Jonah texts again.

"Back at school," from Belle.

Jules writes that she aced her Ring Theory exam, so I send her a trophy emoji and a flexed bicep, plus a donut, bagel, hula hoop, and pool float.

There are a bunch of supportive texts from my friends here. They've met Edi, but they don't really know her. They offer me consolation and meals, a walk, a hug, a glass of wine, whatever I need. "I love you guys so much," I text the group. "We're good. I'll probably just see you on the other side."

Now Jules needs her social security number. "Don't share it with anyone," I write, like a schmo, and she writes back, "oops already posted it on social media." I tell her that she's very funny and she tells me she knows, and that she misses me and Honey and Belle and the cats. I write her back a long message about how her absence feels like an actual hole in my heart, then delete it. "We miss you too," I write, hit SEND.

My parents have texted. "How's Edi?" they want to know. "How are the kids? You? Honey?" I tell them that the kids, Honey, and I are all good, that Edi is so-so. "I mean, how good could she be, I guess?" my dad writes. They can't take it, Edi being sick, while they soldier on healthily in their stubborn, ancient bodies. I know that they can barely even bear to ask after her, though they always do. "Jules screwed up my aol," my dad texts. "I know she was only trying to help, but now I keep getting Mom's emails." "Dad," I text. "You and Mom share an email account." "I'm just saying," he texts back. "I know she didn't mean to." "Are you sleeping at all, sweetie?" my mom writes, and I say, "Totally!" She calls me a liar, then sends me a dozen heart emojis and a sun. "Thanks for checking on us," I write, and put my phone down.

My parents are crazy about Honey now, but they had never seemed completely sure about him when we were first together. "Why is he so even-keeled?" my dad asked once, suspicious and indignant. "And what the hell kind of name is Honey?" I explained how Honey's parents had called him honey in the usual way when he was little— like, "Nighty-night, honey" or "Easy does it, honey, that's a lot of ketchup"—only then the teacher asked his name on the first day of nursery school and he'd said, "Honey." Like, he thought it was his actual name. Since his actual name was Gator, Honey seemed as good a choice as any. ("What the hell kind of name is Gator?" was my dad's somewhat predictable follow-up. This I wasn't completely sure about.) Now that we were split up, though, they'd grown to love him uncomplicatedly. Maybe because he's such a wonderful father. Or because they assume he's blameless in our breakup, which he kind of is.

The short version is that I—surprise!—slept with someone else. But it's messier than that, of course. My high-school boyfriend, a person I had truly, deeply loved when we were seventeen, had been in town for a conference and called me from the hotel. He was newly divorced, and he'd already been flirting with me over email. Then he was here, half a mile away.

I had been feeling catastrophically disconnected from Honey—we seemed to alternate at that time between pointless meta-arguing ("If you would have just said you were sorry instead of blah blah then I wouldn't have had to blah blah blah") and something more like a frozen tundra of arctic silence, and the sled dogs were exhausted and we were out of food and next we were going to be slicing off pieces of each other to roast and eat. The girls were busy being teenagers. Edi had just been diagnosed. Not that that's any excuse, honestly—Edi getting sick. I don't even know if that's part of the reason or not. I just know I got a call from the hotel.

"Hey, Ash," he said, when I picked up, and I said, "Luca. Don't."

He laughed, said, "Don't what?"

"I don't know. Nothing. But don't." I laughed too. I was pacing around my bedroom. "I mean, hi!" I sat on the edge of my bed and pressed my fingertips to my eyelids. When I opened my eyes again, I could see only a gray blur. I could hear Luca smiling.

"Come over," he said—*growled*, really—and I said, "Luca, I can't."

"Oh, you definitely can," he said. I still thought of him as a boy—a boy with a boy's skinny, insatiable body, a boy's wild and fearless heart. "Come to me, Ash."

And I did. I went to him.

And it was just the one time, but I didn't want to be with Honey after. Honey loved me, I knew, but I wanted to be kept up all night, to doze in desire and wake to an astonished somebody tracing their finger down the side of my face. Honey was too rational for that in some ways, and too damaged for it in others. He'd learned not to feel too much growing up, while his mother drank herself to death. He'd learned to look away. He was so warm and accommodating, on the one hand—one of the only husbands I knew who didn't scoldingly turn down the thermostat a dozen times a day. But also, everything he knew about desire he seemed to have learned from old Chevy Chase movies. ("Can I borrow your towel for a sec?" was his classic seduction line when I emerged from the shower. "My car just hit a water buffalo.") Belle and Jules tease him because he has chronically dry eyes and he uses eyedrops called Fake Tears. Whenever he drips them into his eyeballs, they announce, "Uh-oh! Dad's having a pretend feeling!"

I told Honey about Luca and what I'd done, about my loneliness, not feeling loved madly enough. He was briefly unhappy, dragged for a few days, asked no questions, seemed to get over it, was back to whistling "Walking on Sunshine" while he patiently chipped the ice dams off our roof. "Aren't you furious?" I'd pressed, and he shrugged. "I want you to be crazy about me," I'd said, and he said,

"You want that. I know. But you also want space to think and work. Freedom. You want to rest sometimes. You'd hate me if I tried to contain you." He'd sighed, pressed his lips into a thin line. "I love you, but you want impossible things, Ash," he said, finally, and it was true. It still is.

I want impossible things.

CHAPTER 9

The room across the hall is empty today, the crib moved out, a battery-operated votive candle in the doorway signifying this passage. I squinch my eyes shut for a moment, winch my heart open, cover my face with my hands, cover the baby's face in angel stickers, in stars. It's monstrous. It is too much to take. Why do we even do this—love anybody? Our dumb animal hearts.

When Jules was a newborn, I fretted so acutely about her dying that I once thought, *Silver lining—at least if she dies I can stop worrying about her dying*. And by *thought* I mean I said this out loud to Honey, who grimaced, said, "Wow, Ash. Let's see if we can fit a nap into your day." But even right now, if I considered, say, the fact that my legs could be lost in an accident, I'd probably be inclined to saw them off preemptively with a bread knife. It's the anticipation I can't handle. Loss lurks around every corner, and how do we prepare?

"What day is it?" Edi asks after I pull myself together and step into her room, and I have to think. "Thursday?" I say. I unzip my coat. "Friday? Friday."

"No," she says. "What's the date?" There are no clocks here, no calendars. It's like a casino, only without the games or cocktail wait-resses. I look at my phone: It's February twentieth. "I've been here a month," she says, and I say hedgingly, "You have," because I don't know exactly what this means to her. Her face is puffy today, her teeth enormous.

"Did you already write my eulogy?" she asks, and I say, "Edi! No."

"But you've thought about it," she says, and I say, "I don't know. I mean, not exactly."

"Can you please not try to make everyone at my funeral fall in love with you?" she says, not laughing.

"Harsh," I say, instead of *Who even are you?*

"But can you?" she says. "I mean, could you make my eulogy be actually about *me?*"

This may be a reference to my toast at her wedding, which was mostly about what an excellent friend I'd been to Edi, and for so long, and now she was marrying somebody who'd only known her for, like, a minute and who probably couldn't even list her top favorite Jolly Rancher flavors in order (apple, cherry, watermelon), her fa-vorite episodes of *St. Elsewhere*, the only thing she's ever shoplifted (a roll-on bubblegum-flavored lip gloss). Jude and Edi had laughed and laughed, but I worried it had been too much.

"Yes, Edi," I say. "I will make sure your eulogy is about you."

"Will you even remember to mention, like, my career?"

Of course I will! The fact that I already haven't notwithstand-ing! Jude and Edi are both documentary filmmakers—that's actu-ally how they met—and Edi can get pretty much anybody to talk to her: homeless trans kids, death-row prisoners, embattled Supreme Court nominees, children's book authors who were also convicted sex offenders (okay, there was only one of those). I've watched her—the way she speaks quietly and cocks her head to listen, the camera more like a friendly extra limb than an intrusion. "Tell me," she says, and people do. "I'm so sorry," she says, when they cry, and she cries too.

She and Jude once filmed a party I was at, where a famous poet asked everyone how they pictured themselves during the inevitable apocalypse. "You first," he said to me, and I said, "Oh, gosh, wow," before describing myself in a grubby apron, standing over a flaming trash can to roast squirrel kabobs for all the neighborhood kids. "Hmm," he said, in a way that sounded, at least to me, like *so pretty much your regular life, then.* "What about you?" he asked another famous poet, a lovely, soft-speaking person who imagined shooting up and having filthy sex with hot, beefcakey men basically right up until the moment the zombies got him or he died of an overdose. In the film, I look at the camera and say, "Same. That's what I actually meant to say." And you can hear Edi laugh.

"Hey, what's up?" I say now. "Are you having a shitty day?"

"Am I having a shitty day? In hospice? I am, actually!"

So I climb into her bed and tell her about The Cake—the same way, when tiny children are mad or unhappy, you might think to distract them with a little box of raisins. And I'll tell you: Nobody wants a box of raisins when they're furious. Or when they're dying, for that matter. (Does anyone *ever* want a box of raisins?) But Edi does kind of want to hear about The Cake. And what I tell her is that someone named Daisy Goldstar was baking for Dean & DeLuca around the time in question, at least according to Honey's source. "I googled her," I tell Edi. "And it looks like she still has a baking blog. There are cookbooks too. I didn't see anything with polenta, but I sent her an email, so maybe she'll write back."

"I hope you pulled out all the stops," Edi says, and I tell her I did.

"But did you tell her I was dying?" she presses, and I say, "I at least told her it was possible you could die at some point." Edi seems satisfied by this.

"Hey!" I say, leaning over to grab my bag off the floor. "I brought nail polish!" (*Who wants raisins?!*)

"Ooooh!" she says, excited. "Yay! What color? Show me!"

I pull over the wheelie table, line up the bottles. I stopped at the drugstore on my way over, picked out a range of shades—a pearly pink and a classic red, but also a sparkly one, a dark one. "This one," she says. It's the deep slate gray. "Good choice," I say, like a waitress about the squid-ink spaghetti, and she says, "Thank you," and laughs.

Olga peeks in while I'm shaking the bottle. "More *saloon*!" she says. "Ruth might like. You would?"

"Of course!" I say.

Olga leaves and is replaced by Cedar, who asks if Edi's in the mood to hear some music. He doesn't mind about the nail polish and the toxic fumes that are likely to liquefy his brain, which I know because I ask him if he minds. He pulls up lyrics on his phone to sing the Stevie Wonder song Edi requests—"Heaven Is 10 Zillion Light Years Away," a cappella, because he can't figure out the guitar part—and I paint Edi's nails, blow on them, do a second coat.

"I'm so crazily good at this!" I announce, and Edi rolls her eyes, but then looks and says, "You actually are."

Olga wheels Ruth in. "Yes!" I say. "Let's get this party started!"

"Whose party?" Ruth says. "Junior's party?"

"Oh, just this nail polish–and–music party," I say awkwardly, and she shrugs.

I tell Ruth to pick a color, any color, and I'm surprised when she chooses the same nearly black color as Edi. So many of my assumptions about people turn out to be wrong! I try to make a mental note of this.

A college writing teacher once told our class to never describe old people's hands. "It's always going to be a cliché," he said, and then he simpered, "My grandmother's hands! The veins, the skin! So gnarled! I love her! She will die!" As Belle would say: *What a dickhole!* But it kind of stuck, so I'll just mention that Ruth's hands are the hands of an old person. They're so well used that they're actually a little confusing, to be honest—like, where exactly the fingernails begin and end—so I do my best. She closes her eyes while I'm painting, and I can feel every bone in her knuckles even though I'm holding them loosely, like they're baby gerbils I'm afraid of squashing.

"Ta-da!" I say, and she opens her eyes, holds her hands up to look, and then claps. "Marvelous!" she whispers, and then looks again. The clapping has not been kind to her manicure, I see, but she just shakes her head in delight—*Wonder of wonders, miracle of miracles!*—and whispers again, "Marvelous!"

"Darling," she says, and looks deeply into my face. "Would you be so kind as to get me a ginger ale? Diet," she adds. "I'm slimming." Of course! Happily! (Diet? My god.) I dart into the kitchen and pour her soda, stretch the rubber lid over the cup, pop in a bendy straw, and dart back. But there must be some sort of physics principle at play, or some kind of effervescent witchery, because as I'm handing Ruth the cup, ginger ale spews out of the straw all over her white cotton cardigan and terry-cloth slippers. "Fuck!" I say, and then, "Shit. I'm sorry. Fuck! My language. Ugh! I'm so sorry, Ruth." Ruth makes a *pish-posh* motion with her hand, says simply, "You needn't be," blots at the ginger ale with a tissue, and holds up her nails again for everyone to admire.

I paint Cedar's nails next—the pale pink—while Ruth sips what's left of her drink and gossips with Edi about the dogs.

"There you are!" It's Dr. Soprano, filling the doorway. "You weren't in your room," he booms at Ruth. "And hello to the rest of you!" I don't know if all hospice doctors are like this, but ours communicates an expansive lack of urgency. *What's the worst that could happen?* is his vibe—which is oddly comforting to me, though I don't know if his patients feel this way.

"I'm visiting with the young people," Ruth says, and he laughs his big Mafia-don laugh.

"I have to borrow this lady for a minute," he says, and Ruth waves as he wheels her out.

And then here's Jonah, suddenly, red-cheeked, a dusting of snow on his bare, bald head, a happy surprise. "You're here!" Edi says, "Yay!" He tells us that work sucked so he cut out early and drove up. Jonah drives a fancy car that I always think is called a Chivas Regal, which is annoying to him. "You're thinking of Cutlass Supreme," he says, "which is also not the kind of car I drive, on account of I'm not your great-uncle Saul." He kisses both of us, zips out of his coat, tells Edi she looks great, starts unpacking a bag from Russ & Daughters. Not only is there rugelach and bagels and lox and cream cheese, but there is also smoked sable and pickled herring and blini and a tin of caviar that you might reasonably call a *bucket* of caviar. "Jesus, Jonah," I say, "did this thing come with a shovel?"

He shrugs. "I'm rich," he says. "So sue me."

"Do I even like caviar?" Edi says, and we don't know, but we agree that we should find out.

The siren song of lox calls Dr. Soprano back in. "Oooh!" His eyes glitter at the spread. He washes his hands in Edi's sink, dries them, stands there with his expectant face and conspicuously clean fingers until he is invited to help himself and does. He spreads cream cheese on a bagel half and then shingles it thickly with salmon and dots it with caviar. I do the same. For a few minutes there is more eating than talking.

"Is it the *tin can man*?" Edi says, apropos nothing, and we all stop chewing and look at her. She's propped up in bed, nibbling a rugelach and looking back at us like we're abstract art. "In *The Wizard of Oz*," she says.

I shake my head, swallow my last bite of bagel. "I think it's just the Tin Man," I say. "No *can*."

"Is that a thing in real life?" she says, and I say, "I don't think so."

"But there are actually lions and scarecrows and girls and dogs," she says. "Why did they pick one single thing that wasn't a thing?" It's a good question.

"I don't know," I say.

"But you wouldn't just suddenly come upon a tin can man in the woods while you were taking a walk?" she asks. Everyone agrees that no, you wouldn't, and she says, "Phew! That's a relief, right?" Kind of!

I look at Dr. Soprano, who is smiling thoughtfully. He checks Edi's IV. "Let's get some more magnesium into this girl!" he booms, and Jonah says, "Have some lox, Edi. It's the Jewish superfood."

"Nah," she says. "I'm good. One more question, though. Is it called Jamaica or *Croatia*?" That depends! It's called *Jamaica*, it turns out—where their cousin got married. This reminds Jonah to tell the apocryphal story of a great-aunt who flew into Newark and spent a week there thinking it was Manhattan. "Newark, New *York*," Jonah says, imitating her heavy Russian accent. She couldn't find the Empire State Building but had a pretty good time otherwise.

Farrah, meanwhile, is sitting by Edi's bed, staring into her face. "You're a cheese whore," Edi says to the dog, and then to me, "And so are you."

"True," I say. "Just give me a hunk of cheddar and I'll—"

"Hey!" Jonah says. (*Raisins!*) "Edi. There's chocolate! I almost forgot." He digs in his jacket pocket and produces, instead of chocolate, a piece of paper that's been folded and folded into a small, thick square. "Oh," he says. "Wait. I've got a note from Dash."

"Oh!" Edi says, and shakes her head. Jonah is holding out the note, but she doesn't take it. Her eyes fill up, spill over. "No, Jonah."

"Okay," he says. "It's okay. I'll just leave it here for later." Jonah sits on Edi's bed, and she leans against him. "Jonah," she says, and he wraps a long arm around her and says, "I know. I know."

When Edi came up here a month ago, she traveled by ambulance. And before they put her in the ambulance, she'd said good-bye to Dash. Her beautiful, big-eyed, brown-eyed boy. Her baby. The social worker at Sloan Kettering had made a game plan with her, and the idea was to communicate that she would always love him, but also to be somehow crisp and clear about it, to offer that love like it was a heart stamped out of sugar cookie dough, neatly baked and frosted—not a messy anatomical chest full of longing. Full of blood and beating and grief.

"How was it?" I asked Jude when he called me from home, and he said, "About how you'd think, probably." She'd said good-bye to him too, of course—her husband! The person she'd slept beside for tens of thousands of nights; the person she'd shared the most of her jokes with, the most of her radiance. It didn't seem possible! It didn't seem real. ("See ya!" he told me she'd said to him, and he'd laughed through his tears.) But we were both thinking of Dash. We were picturing the Milky Way of mother love filling the sky of Dash's future—galaxies of it, vast and bright and everywhere. So much of it, yes. But so much of it unmappable, unmapped. Unknown.

Not here.

CHAPTER 10

Jonah is still over at Shapely, and Belle has talked me into taking a walk in the woods at the end of our street. It's the best idea anyone has ever had. The sky is a gray Slurpee—so cold and wet that I get a brain freeze when the wind blows. I clutch my head, groaning, and Belle says, "Oh my god, Mama! Can you please not have an actual heart attack?"

"No, no!" I say. "It's good! It's great!"

We see oddly intersecting Vs of geese. Are they coming or going? We can't figure out which way any of them are flying, and we wonder if passing each other gives them an uneasy feeling. We hear them honking, and we imagine they're saying nervously, *Um, guys?*

I point out the willows, already turning golden in the late February light. Belle nods. I tell her about the owl I heard in the night, Thumper and Jelly standing wide-eyed by the window, still as stones.

"Do you think when cats hear an owl, they think of themselves as predators or prey?" Belle asks, and I say I don't know. Maybe a little of both.

"Wait," Belle says suddenly. "Is the thing in your gut flora or fauna?"

"Flora," I say, and she says, "Right. Yeah, I guess gut fauna might be kind of a lot. Like, deer and skunks and whatnot."

We talk a little bit about a piece I'm writing. It's called "Sad Pantry." Belle thinks I've said "Sad Panty" at first, which makes sense, given the sorry state of my underwear. "Is it a *listicle*?" she asks disgustedly, somehow emphasizing the testicular nature of the word. It's not. It's about making dinner out of a single can plus a single dry good. "You know," I say. "Like, tomatoes and rice. Or chickpeas and noodles."

"That's maybe even sadder than the panties," Belle observes. "Though maybe not as sad as your last piece." This is probably true. That piece was called "No Use Crying: Things to Do with Spilled Milk." And it *was* a listicle.

"Any luck on the job front?" I ask. She's looking for something part-time.

"Kind of?" she says. "I think Dad's going to help me get catering work. Everything on Craigslist is just people wanting someone to, like, come and clean their fish tank in the nude."

I laugh. "But how does it pay?" I say.

She moves her hand side to side. "Not as much as you'd hope."

We talk a little about college, which is on Belle's mind. "A year from now, all my applications will be done!" she says. "I mean, knock wood, but how crazy is that?"

She wants to go to a women's school—"What is even the point of being queer otherwise?"—and her dad and I love this idea. At her high school's recent college fair, another mom had sighed and said to me, "Don't you just wish you could do it all over again?" "College?" I'd said. "God. I don't know. I don't think I really have the energy anymore to be date-raped every second." Honey had laughed at least, bless him, while the other mom backed away, presumably into a more normal type of small talk.

"Never leave me," I don't sob now, to Belle. "I know!" I say cheerfully instead. "College! I can hardly believe it!"

We trudge on through the glorious slush, the fresh, metallic air. I'm having a memory of Belle as a toddler in these very woods, running out ahead of Honey and me with her dangly little stringed mittens, her little blue hat with its pompom, and then turning to run back, Honey bending down to scoop her up every time. "Thank goodness you're back!" he said, over and over again. "We missed you!"

I'm also remembering scrolling through pictures on my phone just a few years ago. "Did you take these?" I'd asked Jules. It was a dozen photographs of Honey and me, standing under these trees, fighting. Honey's arms were raised in surrender, palms up. I zoomed in to look at my face—my mouth pulled into a short, grim line, my forehead bunched up like an angry dish towel. I had never seen myself so ugly. "Yeah," Jules said guiltily. "Wow," I said, "I'm sorry you had to see Dad and me fighting like that." "Yeah," she said. "It was really unfun."

It really was. It was the unfunnest.

We watched a documentary once about this famous artist who makes all these beautiful sculptures out of leaves and moss and snow and dirt. It's a thrilling film. You watch him assemble shards of ice into a glittering dome, beach stones into a gray rainbow, sticks into an enormous nest. Everything is gorgeous and ephemeral. And then there's this one scene—like it got cut in from another movie—of him popping home to grab a sandwich. His wife is there, stirring something at the stove, and she's got, like, fifteen tiny children hanging from her like she's a possum. She's fully exasperated, and she says, "Can't you take one of the kids with you?" Very breezily he says that, alas, he cannot. And then it cuts to the next scene where he is *making a sculpture out of dandelions*. Like, he is literally in a meadow picking flowers—this is the work he's doing—and all you can think is, *Really? He couldn't bring one of the kids along?* I'd watched it with Honey. "I hope she leaves him," I said, and he said, "Seriously?" and I felt myself fill with fury like I was a bucket under a tap. Even now, whenever I see one of those famous lichen collages or pebble spirals or whatever, I can still feel all that rage sloshing around. Even the word *wife*. I just picture all of us stirring oatmeal at the stove, knee-deep in everybody's diapers and feelings.

Now Belle is musing aloud about different things:

"Whose idea for a candy flavoring was *horehound*?" she wonders, before concluding that people hate children.

"Did the word *boo-boo* come from *bubo*?" she asks. "Like, during the bubonic plague? Like, *Here, sweetie, it's just a little* bubo, *let Mama kiss it better?*"

She's always thought the expression was *steal* yourself, she explains, "with an *a*," and it never made any sense to her. "I'm always like, 'And put myself *where*?'" I tell her that I just picture being inside a huge, creaky suit of metal armor, and she says she'll picture that too now.

We walk silently for a little while, the sky beyond the woods turning to stripes of blue and white and pink as the sun sets. I stop walking, and Belle stops too. "Hey, Belly," I say, and she turns to face me, her giraffe eyelashes blinking in the narrow strip of face between her black scarf and black watch cap. "I can't figure out if I should be worried about you," I say, and she squints, says briskly, "Yeah, same."

"About *me*?" I say.

"About why you're having sex with so many people."

"It's two people," I say, defensively, and she sighs, says, "Mom, it's at least three. I didn't actually read the whole thing? But I saw a text from Dr. Soprano and it had the word *cock* in it."

"Oh god!" I say, and she says, "Also, I did actually read the whole thing."

"I'm sorry," I say, in lieu of running out of the woods and flinging myself into my car and driving to San Francisco and plunging the car off the Golden Gate Bridge. "That must give you such a gross feeling."

"It does," she says. She shakes her head. "I don't know. It's not the sex, exactly. It's more like obvious kid stuff. I just want you to be with Dad, I guess."

"I know you do," I say. "Your dad's the best. I'm really sorry, Belle."

And she says, "I know you are."

"Way to change the subject, though," I say, and she says, "Right?" and turns to walk home.

We come up the hill into the back of our cul-de-sac, and our little neighbor Robby is there with his plastic sled. "I like your pants!" I say. He's wearing comically too-short striped pajamas above his snow boots. But Belle and I must be unrecognizably bundled because Robby drops his sled and yells, "Stranger danger!"

"Robby!" I call. "It's us!" But he is already bolting up the street, tugging open his front door, and disappearing into his house.

"Oh my god, Mom." Belle is laughing so hard she squats down. "I think I'm actually peeing. *I like your pants?*" I'm laughing so hard I'm crying. "What is my problem?" I say, and she shakes her head and scoops up Robby's sled. "Maybe text his mom?" she says, and I say, "Good idea."

"Seriously, though," I say, after I write a quick apology to our neighbor and Belle and I are peeling off layers in our kitchen. "What is wrong with me?" I am so tired suddenly I have to stop myself from lying down on the floor.

"Come here," Belle says, and holds open her arms, the way I always have for her. One's own comforting child! It's too much. "You're okay," she says. I'm crying a little into her neck. "This is just really hard," she says. "And sometimes it's important for children"—she pulls back to look at me, laughing again—"to be stranger-dangered by a friendly neighbor."

CHAPTER 11

It's bitterly cold again. Our little house is fringed in icicles, and Honey has had to come and jump-start my twenty-year-old Chevrolet. "I'm sorry," I said when he pointed questioningly at Jonah's massive, fancy Cutlet Supreme or whatever the fuck it is. "Neither of us has jumper cables."

"Not a problem," Honey said. He handed me a bag with stuff for Edi, then kissed my cheek, threw a handful of salt onto the icy driveway, and drove back to the dispensary.

Now I'm back at Shapely, rubbing some peppermint-scented CBD cream into Edi's feet, feeling saintly about myself because of it.

"Magma?" Edi says, and I say, "What?"

She shakes her head.

"Mama?" I say. "Your mom?"

"Magma," she says.

"Like, molten lava?" I say, and she shakes her head.

"Like what I graduated," she says. "*Magma* cum laude?"

"Um, that was me," I say. "You actually graduated *summa* cum laude. But it's *magna*."

She nods, says, "Jonah's here?" and I shake my head.

"He had to go back to New York. He'll come up again on Friday."

"Who are those guys, then?" she says, and points out the window. "Hey, guys!" she says shyly, waving.

"*Which* guys?" I say, and she points again. Out her window, the leafless trees are swaying in the wind.

"Those waving guys," she says.

"Ah!" I say. "I'm not sure." She nods.

"That stuff Honey sent over is good," she says, stretching and happy, and I say, "Isn't it!" The truth is that I don't actually know, since I've stopped getting high. The last time I smoked with Honey I just sat around in a stoned panic wondering aloud about how the drug ever gets out of your system, *if* it ever does. "But the blood-brain barrier . . ." I'd wondered abstractly, and Honey said dryly, "This is fun!" But he laughed anyway, and held me until I felt okay enough to eat some Caesar salad and watch people renovating their lake houses on TV.

I ask Edi if she remembers the first time we got stoned. We were in Central Park with Luca and a friend of Edi's, her cooler friend Alice, about whom I harbored—and still harbor—an unholy jealousy. While I continued snorting popcorn out of my nose to *Caddyshack*, Alice had introduced Edi to the kinds of movies that were called *films*, and during which people arrived at the dinner table naked and oinking, wearing only diamond necklaces and pig masks; whenever I went with them, I peeked sideways at their faces in the darkened art-house theater, hoping to glimpse the kind of bafflement or dismay that never actually flickered into view. "Breathtaking," they'd say after, and I'd be all "Dang! One hundred percent!" In Sheep Meadow, we'd spread out an old tablecloth, eaten slabs of watermelon soaked in vodka, and passed around a joint Alice had stolen from her dad's stash—he was some kind of music executive, and their house was always filled with drugs. It was a gorgeous late spring day, blossoms fluttering from all the trees like confetti, the sun beaming down on us like love itself, and I celebrated our youth, our ripe freedom, this intoxicating age of Aquarius, by becoming deranged with anxiety and then falling asleep, waking only to barf pinkly into a Tupperware full of fruit rinds.

Edi shakes her head. "Not really," she says, and then, "Wait, did you get a sunburn on your ass?"

"Wow," I say. "Not that I know about!"

She shakes her head again, mutters mysteriously, "I think I'm thinking of your wedding."

At the risk of sounding like a diamond commercial, we share a lifetime of memories, Edi and I. We went to preschool together and then elementary school. I wore green corduroy knickers and a Gunne Sax blouse to her bat mitzvah. We trick-or-treated together, were flashed together in Central Park by a man in an actual trench coat, made ribbon-braided barrettes together. We attended different high schools, but we went to REM concerts together, to David Bowie concerts. We ate mocha-chip Frusen Glädjé. We drank Tab and Fresca and diet Slice, spritzed each other with Anais Anais. We kept toothbrushes at each other's houses, showed each other our hickeys and hurt feelings, our SAT scores and pregnancy tests. She ended up at Columbia and I ended up here for college, but we went abroad to Italy the same semester of junior year, swallowed our own body weight in gnocchi, and stayed overnight at a brothel in Naples, which we had mistaken for a youth hostel. We presided over each other's weddings, hosted each other's baby showers. We held each other's newborns, and then, during her treatment and my separation, each other's hands and hearts.

Edi's memory is like the backup hard drive for mine, and I have that same crashing, crushing feeling you have when the beach ball on your computer starts spinning.

I have the feeling you'd have if there were a vault with all your jewels in it, everything precious, only the person with the combination to the lock was hanging on to a penthouse ledge by a fingertip.

"Hey." Edi's got her shirt yanked up, and she's looking at her PEG tube, blinking slowly. "Does this look okay to you?" It does not!

I talk to Violet at the nurses' station, explain that the insertion site looks angry and infected. I ask if I can get a bottle of sterile water to irrigate it. They've got their hands full today. A new patient is so aching and agitated that they've wheeled her out of her room and brought her up next to the desk to comfort her—the way you might bring your sick kid into bed with you. Violet is smoothing this woman's pale hair gently back from her ancient, clenched face even while she's simultaneously filling out paperwork and, also, talking to me. She sighs, looks up. "We're actually out of sterile water," she says. "But Ash, I think you can just use tap water. I don't think it really makes too much difference." She does not add "at this point," but I hear the words hanging there all the same.

"Violet," I say, and my eyes are filling with tears. She stands up, puts her arms around me over the desk. "Ash. I know. But just refill the sterile bottle from the tap. You don't need to mention it to Edi," she says. "Do you want me to do it?" she asks, and I tell her, "No, no. I'm good. I've got it."

Edi's freezing after we flush out her tube, so I turn up the heat, pile blankets onto her, wind my cashmere scarf, which I have borrowed from Jonah, around her neck. "Better," she says. "Here." She holds out her phone. It's a picture Jude has sent of Dash holding out a newly lost tooth, smiling his gappy smile.

"Oof," I say, and she says, "Right? It's a little . . . heartrendering."
She looks at me uncertainly. "*Lard* rendering?" she says.

"Heartrending," I say, and she laughs.

"Oh my god," she says. "My brain."

Edi eats part of a brownie and a quart of watermelon cubes, drinks
two enormous glasses of apple juice, then dozes under her many blankets. I text back and forth with Jules, who is in the mood to remind
me about the time I made her write a thank-you note to each of her
friends who'd come to her sixteenth birthday party. They'd given her
a group gag gift, which was a dildo. "You actually made me write
thank you for the dildo," she texts now, which is not precisely true
(I'd suggested she just say *gift*), but it's close enough. She adds a
dozen laugh-crying emojis. "So far this is by far the best part of my
day," I text her truthfully.

"Are you at school?" I text Belle—disingenuously, since the school
has already robocalled to the contrary—and she writes, "Yes," and
then, a few seconds later, "Actually, no." I send her a quizzical emoji,
which she ignores.

"What the fuck is with all the farmhouse sinks?" she texts instead.

My parents have texted their worry about everyone; Jude has asked
for updates; Jonah has written some more thoughts about electrolytes
and also that he loves me. I'm so tired I feel like I've been poisoned
by a fairy-tale witch.

"Hey, Ash." Dr. Soprano has stuck his head in the door and is
boom-whispering. "Can I talk to you for a second?" I smile tiredly,
and he says, "No, really talk," and I say, "Of course," and follow
him out.

"I've added some more Ativan to her IV," he tells me in the hallway. "For the anxiety, and something called Haldol, which might help
her think a little more clearly." I nod. "I'm not sure what's going on,

exactly—we're waiting on new blood work—but we might be seeing the start of what we call a *change in status*." I nod again. "You never know, of course," he says, "I mean, Edi! She's a tough nut. But I'm sorry, Ash." He folds me into his enormous arms, pulls me against his enormous torso, and for a minute I am comfortingly unable to see or hear or even breathe all that well. Is this what a sensory deprivation tank is like? Maybe that's what I need! "Thank you," I say, pulling back. I use my sleeves to dry my face, to dry his sweater vest.

Somewhere in the house, a handful of sad Ukrainian Jews are being evicted from Anatevka, their *intimate, obstinate* hometown shtetl. "Soon I'll be a stranger in a strange new place," they sing. Dr. Soprano shrugs. "Then again," he says, "I'm the one who gave Ruth two weeks." He laughs.

"We simply don't know," he says, and I say, "I know. Not knowing seems to be all I know anymore."

CHAPTER 12

Now it's later that same day, and Edi has rallied. I'd popped home while she slept, fed Belle and the cats, looked away from the growing pile of unopened mail, and then returned "for a nightcap," as we like to say about bedtime visits to Shapely. Edi was sitting up in bed when I arrived, in a clean white robe, freshly showered, leafing through the *New Yorker*. A fancy candle was sending out fragrant plumes of sandalwood and fig from her tray table.

"Hey!" I say. "You're a sight for sore eyes!"

"I feel good," she says. "That new nurse came in and actually managed to help me take a dump." This nurse, it turns out, is a retired civil engineer who ended up back in school for nursing because she felt like all her hydraulic problem-solving was going to waste. "She basically had, like, a bullet-list game plan," Edi says. "It was a whole methodology. She was like, *Rest assured, at the end of this there will be feces.*"

"Wow!" I say. "I'm impressed."

I've been thinking lately that if death were an opera, the villain would be a character named *Constipatio*. Everyone else would sing soaringly of these distilled final days of consciousness, the content of a life well lived, and then he would come onstage and groan his evil basso arias about clogging discomfort and humiliation. "I love you all, but I have to go and grunt out one final tiny turd!" are basically everybody's last words.

"I feel like you should either be dying and feel good," Edi says now, "or you should be in pain but getting better. It's not fair to feel shitty *and* die."

"That is so not fair," I agree.

"But I've felt worse, so." She shrugs, smiling. "Speaking of—hey, pass me those prunes, would you?"

I do, then take them back from her so I can eat one too. "Naturally occurring objects such as pit, twig, shell, or stem fragments may occur," I read from the bag. "Okay, I'm not in love with the repetition of *occur*, obviously. But also? All that crap doesn't just *occur* in the bag. Like, it gets negligently *left behind*."

"Are you going to end up writing about this?" Edi asks. "Don't."

"Maybe," I say. "We'll have to see. And also, sorry to change the subject, but this?" I point to a new bouquet. It's massive—like something you would see in the lobby of a museum, arranged in a stone bathtub they'd exhumed from the pyramids—and it's gorgeous: pussy willows, lilies, roses, something silver and ferny.

"Jonah," Edi says, by way of explanation, and I say, "Wowza," rub my fingers and thumb together in the universal sign of *That bouquet must have cost a fortune.*

"Hey," Edi says, shy suddenly. "Can I ask you something?"

If it's *Are you shagging my brother?* I decide I'm going to fall onto the carpet and fake having a stroke.

"Of course," I say. I pull my chair closer to the bed and sit.

"What do you think happens after you die?" she says.

"Oh!" I say. "Gosh."

I was raised in a fully atheist household, so *not much* is the short answer. "Just toss me in the dumpster when I go!" my dad likes to announce, and when I'm like, "Um, Dad, I think funerals are actually more about—" he interrupts me. *"In the dumpster!"* "Okay!" I say. "The dumpster it is!"

When the girls were little, they were confused about whether people believed that heaven existed in the sky—like, the *earth's* sky. This was legitimately confusing, actually. "Is it heaven just for this planet or for the whole universe?" they'd wondered. "I guess the whole universe?" I said, and they countered with many picky questions about clouds, pearly gates, angels sitting around in the blue, no dark matter in sight, and I realized that everything I knew had probably come from a Gary Larson comic. Or maybe an episode of *Looney Tunes*.

"I believe there's some kind of energy," I say now. I am winging it! "Something that's not exactly you? But that's, like, not *not* you." Edi nods politely. "Like, it's halfway between people's memories of you and something that's more like a material fact." This I might actually believe. "Some kind of animate stardust." *What?* "Maybe you turn into a kind of free-floating consciousness that surrounds the people you love so that you're kind of there with them still and the air they breathe is somehow made out of you." Edi smiles—she's probably picturing all of us coughing and wheezing out a lungful of her consciousness. I'm such an asshole. "I'm sorry," I say, "I can hear that I'm not making any sense. I guess I'm not sure what I think—besides that the people we lose stay with us somehow. What do you think?"

"I really don't know," she says. "I feel like you just described more about your experience after I die than mine. Will I *be* somewhere? With my own sense of myself?" I don't know—I hope so. "It's so frustrating that I'm stuck in this stupid, sick body," she says. "It seems so inessential, somehow, but then, there's really nowhere else for me to go." I picture unzipping my own body and wrapping her inside of it, like a shared coat.

"I would give anything to keep you," I say through the sob that's gathering in my throat, and she says, "I know you would. I would give anything to stay."

"Soon I'll be a stranger in a strange new place," I sing to her, and she closes her eyes, smiles.

"Mostly," she says, "I'm just really, really thirsty." The body and its petty demands! Grief is crashing over our heads like a tsunami, this miraculous soul is about to be homeless, but thirst is thirst. So I fill her night—this one, beautiful night, the only here and now we've ever got—with Sprite.

CHAPTER 13

I'm still on my back with my knees up, but my gynecologist has wheeled her little stool around by my head to talk to me.

"Ash, everything looks good. I really don't think you have cervical cancer or ovarian cancer or even—What did you call it?—*vag* cancer. I know your friend is sick. It is so, so worrying."

I've heard the verb *leaking* used about tears before, but maybe I've never really understood it until now. My eyes—they're like cruddy old faucets. I'm not even crying, not really, but tears are nonetheless running down into my hair. I feel like a sculpture of myself that's been cast in lead. If I had a million dollars, I would pay it just to lie here for the rest of the day, with my head on this crinkly little pillow.

"Okay," I say.

Her eyes are green beacons of concern. "I'm happy to order some blood work," she says, "if that will reassure you."

Marry me, I don't say. I just say, "No. I don't know. It's fine. Also, I should have mentioned this before, I'm whoring a little bit." She smiles, asks if I'm being safe. I tell her I am. "But I'm really, really tired," I say. "Like, *clinically* tired. Maybe I have a deficiency."

"I think we might call that deficiency *grief*," she says gently. "Although a B complex wouldn't kill you."

She hugs me, tells me to take care of myself, and I leave with a blister pack of something, a vitamin prescription, and a handful of the lube samples and condoms I grab from the bowl like a sleazy trick-or-treater.

Back in the car, I look through all my tapes. One nice thing about my elderly sedan is that it has an actual tape deck. I have every mix-tape Edi ever made me, and I pop one in now to amplify my sadness. It's a tape called "Ashes to Ash" (written in bubble letters, naturally), and Roxy Music's "Avalon" comes on first to ruin me. Life is just see-sawing between the gorgeous and the menacing—like when you go for a run and one minute the whole neighborhood is lilacs in purple bloom, and then the next it's stained boxer shorts and an inside-out latex glove.

I'm driving and crying, and then there are lights behind me—How long have they even been there?—a police car. I pull over a little to let it pass, but it pulls in behind me. Shit! I watch in my side mirror as the cop gets out of his car, walks up to mine. I hold up my finger— *One sec!*—because I have to use pliers to grab the broken stem of the window crank and turn it.

"Do you know the speed limit on this street?" he says, and then, "Oh, hey, now." I'm crying, my face in my hands along with the pliers. "Okay, okay. Nothing bad is going to happen here. I just need to see your license and registration."

I have literally never been pulled over before. It's not saying much, really. Honey taught me how to drive when I was pregnant with Jules, and in the twenty years since, I've driven like the kind of grandma who takes the car out once a week to go shopping for soup bones.

I find my license in my wallet, then open the glove compartment, where there is a giant stack of papers. What are all these papers? I pull them out. "Is it this?" I say. I'm crying so hard I can barely see. "No," he says. "That's an oil change. Nope. That one's tires. That's a takeout menu. Here, let me look."

"My friend is dying," I sob, "over at Shapely. The Graceful Shepherd. I'm running a little late. I have to bring her this lip balm and this bottle of lemonade. And these socks."

The cop looks at me without speaking. "And also?" I'm still crying. "That *People* magazine."

"Okay, okay," he says. His breath makes a little puff of white every time he speaks. He takes the pile from me into his leather-gloved hands, finds my registration, looks at it quickly, places it on top, and hands everything back to me. "That's hard, what you're doing. I hear that. I'm just going to let you go with a warning today, okay?"

"Thank you," I say, crying. "But you should do whatever you need to do. I don't want to just be, like, this crying entitled white lady in the middle of your day who doesn't get a ticket."

"Well, I don't know you, but today, yeah, that's pretty much what you are. Good luck with your friend."

He walks back to his car and gets in, and I wait for him to pull out so that I can cry some more and then, hopefully, die here, but his car doesn't move. I call Honey, who picks up on the first ring, "Hey, Ash," he says. "Everything okay?"

I cry-explain that I've been pulled over in town, that there's a cop waiting behind me, that I can't pull myself together enough to drive. "Just hang on," he says. "You're only a block from me."

I married a person who just wants to say yes to everything, and I basically forced him to say no to our marriage. How did this happen? Pretty much the only thing Honey doesn't like is a to see a semi cab driving on the highway with no truck attached, which simply, as he puts it, gives him a *weird feeling*. But that's the extent of his antipathies. The first time I was on an airplane with him, Honey was even riveted by the routine safety presentation. "Do you think the flight attendants have to learn to mime more broadly?" he'd wondered. "Or only those very specific clicking and inflating actions?" He pointed to the illustrated safety instructional card in our seat pocket. "Tell me she's having a bad time," he said. It was a woman in a skirt suit and heels, zooming down the inflatable slide with what you could only call a mad grin on her face.

Waiting to taxi, we studied the *SkyMall*, picking out favorite things from every page. Much later, we would do this with the girls too, who always surprised us with their odd little wants: a feather duster on a pole for cleaning chandeliers; a heated dog bed; moisturizing gloves; a pear-shaped basket for pears. But Honey wanted what I'd thought he'd want: poolside robots and money-counting gadgets and tools that did chores for you automatically so you wouldn't have to do them yourself. Especially given how little wealth he seemed interested in amassing, Honey was not a person looking to avoid the good life.

We were flying to Edi and Jude's wedding, and, once we were aloft, Honey held my hand and leaned into me to see out the window. "Look!" Far below us, a bridge twinkled in the deep blue evening like twinned strings of fairy lights. The sun was setting on the horizon in watercolor bands. All around us, passengers were dozing or leafing through the in-flight magazine, while my whole body hummed with the magic of flight, the magic of this person beside me who was whispering, as the beverage cart approached, "Order Bloody Mary mix. You'll feel like you got free gazpacho." Honey was like a quiet, one-man party—a fun one, with really good food.

Now, by the time he comes loping up the street, the cruiser has pulled out and driven off. Honey climbs into the passenger side and hugs me awkwardly over the gearshift. "The cop left after all," he says, and I say, sheepish, "Yeah. I told him my husband was coming to rescue me."

"But did you tell him your husband was *patiently* coming to rescue you *again*?" I cry and nod. He smiles, hands me a tissue, says he'll drive me over to Shapely, peek in on Edi with me. "You're the best," I say, and he laughs and says, "I really am."

CHAPTER 14

Edi's in the shower when we arrive, so Honey and I kill some time foraging around the kitchen. "Who made short ribs?" he says, his head in the fridge. He's impressed. A volunteer has baked corn muffins, and we decide to split one, which Honey insists on griddling first while I make a fresh pot of coffee. The muffin is buttery, crisp-edged, and delicious, the coffee rich and good, since I've poured a thick layer of cream into each of our mugs.

The hospice fridge is filled with cream: ice cream, sour cream, heavy cream, cans and cans of whipped cream. There's definitely a *now or never* feeling about food around here, and it makes you wonder what you think you might be waiting for in your own life. I mean, crusty, gooey mac and cheese? Thickly frosted éclairs? Velveeta melted over a plate of potato chips—what the nurses call the *house nachos*? Eat your kale and blueberries and whatever else, but go ahead. Have some of the good stuff now too.

We unload clean dishes from the dishwasher, pop in our plates and cups, wander back to check on Edi, who's sitting cross-legged on her bed, working on a crossword puzzle. She's wearing a fluffy pink sweater, white underpants, and white thigh-high compression stockings.

"I'm sorry, what are you—in a Bon Jovi video?" I say, and she laughs. "You look weirdly hot."

When I bend to kiss her, she studies my face for an extra beat. "Were you crying?" she says, and I say, "No." She shakes her head, scowls. "Anyways," I say, "I have news about The Cake!"

I tell her and Honey that I've heard back from Daisy Goldstar. Yes, she was indeed the baker of the Sicilian lemon polenta pound cake, which she referred to immodestly as "my signature cake, a FAMOUS cake." No, she cannot share the recipe. She understands that we really, really want it—and she understands why. Instead, she has asked for Edi's address, and said to keep our eyes peeled for a surprise.

"Bitch recipe hoarder," Edi says, "But also, oh my god! What a sweetheart! Do you think she's sending an actual cake?" I do! When, exactly, that cake will get here is a question I have tried not to think too much about. "Wow," Edi says. "This really is kind of a dream come true! I can't wait. We should get a bottle of champagne." This is an excellent idea. We definitely will.

Honey leaves to return to work, and Cedar pops his head in. He's heading out for the day, but has time for one quick song. "Just come and talk to us for a minute," Edi says. "Take a load off. Sit. Here." She gestures at her table, her dresser. "There's candy all over the place. Regular and irregular. Help yourself."

"I'm good," Cedar says. "Thanks." He puts his guitar case down, pulls up a chair, and sits.

"I have a question," Edi says. "What's the deal with the Wu-Tang Clan?"

"Say more?" Cedar says politely.

"I don't know. They just don't seem so great. I mean, 'Dance Hall Days'? Please."

"You're thinking of Wang Chung," I say. "A new-wave band from the eighties," I explain to Cedar. He pulls up "Protect Ya Neck" on his phone so we can listen.

"*This* is Wang Chung?" Edi says, and I laugh, say, "*Wu-Tang Clan*," accuse her of becoming her own grandma. She laughs too. "But, like, actually," she says.

"Well, you've kind of always been like this," I say consolingly. I remind her of the time Honey said he had to go and smoke some hearts of palm, and Edi, questioningly, had pantomimed putting a doobie to her lips.

"I'm sorry," she says, "but aren't you the person who eavesdropped on your mum and her Dublin cousin gossiping about somebody's hysterectomy and thought for years that The Troubles in Ireland were *gynecological*?" This is true. "And also?" She's rolling now. "Ash is the person who thought the Rotary Club met to talk about the flow of traffic."

"Okay, Professor McSmartypants," I say. "What *is* the Rotary Club?"

She grimaces. "It's not about . . . rototillers," she says uncertainly.

After Cedar leaves, a nursing assistant named Kirby steps into the room, closes the door behind her, stands in front of the closed door, talks loudly to us about the forecast—snow!—and asks if Edi has a favorite song to play for her on her phone; she's dying (*Dying!*) to learn about new music! Edi shrugs and puts on Josephine Baker singing "La Vie en Rose," and Kirby asks her to turn it up.

Ah, right! Everything clicks. This is Shapely protocol for transporting a dead person from the house—what they call "finalizing a passage." They shared this morale-maintenance system with Honey and me at Edi's intake. A staff member or volunteer comes into each room to distract everybody while the morgue folks are here, and, except for not being funny, it's got all the makings of a sitcom mishap: people tiptoeing around with a finger to their lips, the body snuck out of the building under a cheerful bedspread, nothing to see here, folks! This is a place where people come to *live*! I love them for so tenderly trying to protect their patients.

"Who died?" Edi says after Kirby leaves. I'm not actually sure. I hope it's not Junior or Ruth, since a) I love them, and b) I've convinced myself that Edi won't die before they do. So everyone has to live forever.

"Oh my god," she says suddenly, brightening. "Remember Edinburgh?"

After college, Edi and I had flown to England, first to visit my grandparents in Sheffield, and then to ride a train up to Scotland, where we spent a wonderful week walking a path called the West Highland Way. Somewhere along this Way, over pints of ale in a pub, we got to talking with a splendid woman from Edinburgh, who invited us to stay with her on our way back down—her kids were grown and she had a spare bedroom to stick us in. This was well before cell phones, so we showed her our train tickets and she wrote down the information. "Lovely!" she'd said (*loovly*). "I'll see you then!" And sure enough, there she was at the train station a week later, throwing up her arms when she saw us and bustling us cheerfully to her tiny car, wedging our packs in the trunk.

She asked about the rest of our trip, and we told her about the haggises boiling in the hostel kitchens, about the rain and the misty lochs and our blistered feet. Then she pulled up in front of a row of small brick houses, turned the engine off. "I'm afraid I've a bit of awkward news," she said, unbuckling her seat belt and turning to look at us. "Me dad's died, and he's laying in at the house."

Oh my god! we said. We were so sorry! Here she'd picked us up, and we'd just been yakking away, oblivious. Please, we said, let us find a hostel or a B and B. She wouldn't hear of it. Besides, there was plenty to eat and drink, and good company too. And so, still wearing our grubby shorts and hiking boots, we joined a party taking place around an open coffin. A wake. We ate mutton pie and drank scotch, and we listened and laughed while these people we didn't know shared their memories with us of this blue-suited man—their friend, brother, father, grandpa, uncle, cousin, neighbor—whom we would never, exactly, meet.

Later, our new friend made us up a bed in the room next to the living room, where her father was dead. Edi and I stayed awake all night, terrified, laughing and laughing as quietly as we could. We may or may not have competed in a "most convincing corpse" contest—who can say? Death was sad and scary, but we were twenty-two years old. We were going to live forever.

I tell Edi that of course I remember Edinburgh, but that now I'm having another memory too—a story I was recently telling the girls to illustrate some point I'd been making about life before cell phones. The semester Edi and I were in Italy, we'd gone off to different places for spring break—she was meeting her boyfriend somewhere, and I was visiting a new friend in Sicily—but we made a plan to meet up and ferry together to the island of Capri. Only we couldn't figure out where the ferry terminal was, exactly—it wasn't in our *Let's Go!* guide—so we unfolded a paper map, picked the unnamed end of a peninsula, and agreed on a date and time to meet.

On the appointed day, I got off the bus in Sorrento, not far from the spot we'd picked, and walked hesitantly down a long path that ended at a cliff over the sea. Edi wasn't there, of course. Why hadn't we just agreed we'd meet at the ferry terminal, wherever it turned out to be? Was this even the right date? Should I travel across to Capri or return to Florence? We didn't have a backup plan. I ate half of the enormous tuna sandwich I'd brought to share, oil dripping all over me from the good fish and the marinated peppers, and tried to think. I checked my watch one last time, took a long swig of wine from my canteen, packed up the end of my lonely picnic, and stood to walk back. And there she was! Edi! Waving to me from the path, like a mirage hobbled by an enormous backpack.

If there's a metaphor for our friendship, it might be this. The blind faith. The absolute dependability. The love like a compass, its north always true.

"As I recall, you'd already eaten the sandwich you'd brought me," Edi says now.

"Oh my god, I so didn't!" I say. "I saved half of it for you! That's, like, the best part of the story!"

"Potato, po-tah-to," she says, and smiles at me. "But it was pretty epic either way."

CHAPTER 15

It's the next day. Edi's asleep, and I have my laptop out. I'm ghost-writing someone's memoir about amnesia, and it's pretty much as difficult and dully comedic as it sounds. "Tell me more about that," I say, digging for details during our weekly video meeting, and he says, "I really can't recall!"

"Could it be kind of high-concept?" Belle asked recently. "Like, a blank book that could double as a journal for other amnesiacs? And *nobody ever writes in it?*" (Belle is the same person, I should mention, who had the idea for a nihilist yard sale. People would come and you would charge them five dollars for the pleasure of *not* buying half a scented candle or a used fondue set. "Think how happy they'll feel when they drive away!" was her thinking. "They got all that nothing for only five bucks!")

To complicate matters, the amnesiac is also prone to self-aggrandizing exaggeration. "I stowed away on a boat once," he told me, before describing his shanty-singing months as a kind of vaga-bond hobo deckhand. When I asked what the boat had been called, he said, sheepish, "Actually, the whole experience was called Dartmouth Semester at Sea."

Maybe the memoir will be called *Lies I Can't Quite Remember*.

"What are you working on?" Edi's awake, so I tell her. While I'm talking, she drinks noisily through a straw from an enormous glass of something, shakes her head, sighs. "Why do you do this shit, Ash?" she says, and I'm offended, so I say, offendedly, "Sorry I need to support my family."

I hate ghostwriting so much that I charge outrageously for it in the hopes that nobody will hire me. But then anyone who does hire me is willing to pay a fortune, so I almost never say no. But then the whole premise self-selects the worst clients: rich men who are in love with their own story (or whatever they remember of it) and spray it out at me like silly string, like shaving cream. I'm covered in sticky webs and puddling gobs of their foamy white recollections and they're jetting off to a private island, yelling back to me over the noise of the engine, "Now go turn that into a bestseller!"

"Why don't you write your own book?" Edi says. "You have a *PhD*, for fuck's sake, Ash." This is true, though not super relevant in my opinion. "All your sweetheart underachiever bullshit is not aging well."

"Wow," I say. "Okay. Geez." I don't know if pain and grief and dying are turning Edi into a person who feels this way about me—or if she's always felt this way, and hospice is turning her into a person who doesn't bother not sharing that fact. I remind myself not to tell her about the women's health piece I'm working on, tentatively titled "No Cuntry for Old Vaginas."

"So you don't want to hear about how Sun-Maid invited me to be a raisin ambassador?" I say, and she laughs. "I just have to write fifteen *raisin-centric*—their term—blog posts. And, in return, well—there's no money, but they fly me to Fresno for the annual raisin harvest and the crowning of the Raisin Queen? And everyone gets a year's supply of raisins. Which, in my family, is zero raisins."

"Tell me you're not doing that," Edi says.

"I'm not doing that," I say.

"Oh my god, but are you actually?" she says, and I say truthfully, "I am actually not."

"Write a book about *this*," Edi says.

"About us?" I say "Friendship?"

"Yeah," she says. "About all of this. Death too. About dying. Hospice."

"No," I say. "I would never finish that book. I would never want it to end. I would just keep writing and writing it forever." I am trying to not cry.

"Just get in and get out," she says, and lies back, closes her eyes. "Wait. Am I thinking of Anne Rice or Ayn Rand?" she says, and I say, "Ayn Rand."

The volunteer coordinator sticks her head in to let us know that a fifth-grade group is at the home to play a recorder concert and would we like to attend?

"Would we!" Edi says, then, "I don't know. *Would* we?"

"We would!" I say.

Out in the living room, some of the Shapely folks are sitting on the couches and some in wheelchairs and armchairs, a few staff members standing around at the edges. There are lots of family members too—everybody mustering a bit of weary cheer for these kids who shuffle in and stand in a nervous semicircle, clutching their terrible instruments. The music teacher introduces the first song—it's "Hot Cross Buns," natch—and the students blow out the notes like they're blowing out trick birthday candles. *Huff huff huff. Huff huff huff.* I'm remembering a long-ago recorder concert of Jules's, and how Belle could hardly pull herself together to watch because we'd stopped at the supermarket on the way—we were in charge of bringing milk and cookies—and somebody was restocking the dairy case *from behind*!

This was a particular terror of Belle's in those days—matched only by the wrinkly first sheets of toilet paper stuck down on the full roll—and she clutched us, wide-eyed, as we saw yogurts push forward in their rows, as we glimpsed a hand. "Who's back there behind the yogurt?" she asked in the car. "And why don't they come around to the front?" "Belle, honey," Jules said soothingly, "it's just the way they do it."

And, despite my lengthy reminiscence, here at Shapely, the recorder concert *is still going on*! They huff out the first notes of "We Shall Overcome"—*huff huff huff huff huuuff-huff-huff*—and Edi reaches for my hand. "Remember?" she whispers, and I do. When Dash was in kindergarten, I'd gone down to Brooklyn for a Special Friends Day in his classroom, and we'd sung this song together. Afterward, the teacher had asked the kids if they knew what *overcome* meant. Little hands shot up. Like, *all* the hands. "Yes—Axel?" "Like, when a friend comes to your house for a playdate?" "Ah," the teacher had said, smiling. "You're thinking of *come over*—and you're right. That's exactly what *come over* means." She explained a little bit about overcoming, spoke gently of civil rights, asked the kids if they had any more thoughts. All the hands shot back up: "Well, one time? The battery fell out of my mom's phone? Like, suddenly! And then she put it back in." "This is some epic Nobel Prize shit," Edi had whispered to me. The rest of the kids catalogued similar resiliencies: a broken candy dish glued back together; spilled cornmeal swept into a dustpan; toothpaste blooped onto somebody's slipper and then wiped away with a square of toilet paper.

Now this soaring ballad of resistance just brings to mind a smattering of inconsequential domestic mishaps. "Deep in my heart," Jude still likes to sing, "I do believe . . . that goldfish can be flushed away." I'm thinking now, though—about how quiet Dash was, sitting in my lap then. Edi was already sick, although they hadn't told him. But maybe he'd known? Maybe *overcome* meant something different to him already. Or maybe he was just thinking about robots or butterscotch pudding. You really never know.

The song comes to its rousingly huffed conclusion. Edi's head is on my shoulder now, and I squeeze her hand. But she's fast asleep. The audience claps, the musicians bow, juice and frosted oatmeal cookies are put out and consumed, and the room empties slowly. It's just Edi and me and lots of fake flowers and real plants and inspirational sayings. THE WAY TO HAVE A FRIEND IS TO BE ONE, reads a needlepoint pillow on the couch. True! GOOD LUCK! reads a helium balloon, floating up by the ceiling. *Good luck dying!*

CHAPTER 16

Scriv and Belle are in Belle's room, and the door is closed. They're laughing quietly, and it's as pure a sound as jingle bells or rainfall. I picture flinging open the door, catching them at whatever it is they're doing, shouting, "Touché!"

I hear Scriv giggling, Belle's low voice teasing, "Meat lover."

I'm just back from the dermatologist, where I tried unsuccessfully to be diagnosed with skin cancer. Instead, the doctor, who is not famous for acting like, or maybe even *being*, a person, gestured at my body to the nurse, who was taking notes. "Moderate sun damage on the upper chest," he said to her, and then to me, "That's from not wearing sunscreen."

"Ugh," I said. "I'm sorry."

"Oh, don't be," he said. "I don't care."

I laughed. "I don't think *not caring* is what you want to project. I mean, I'm sure you *care*."

And he said, unsmiling, "I really actually don't." I raised my eyebrows and winked at the nurse, and she laughed.

The fact that Belle is unlikely to end up dating some feelingless robot is striking me as the greatest blessing I can imagine. Even her gentle father! "What if you came home and I was dead on the floor?" I asked him once, pissed about something or other. "What would you do?" "Um," he said, but I interrupted before he could answer. "You would step around me, whistling 'Dancing Queen.' Then you'd make guacamole or feed the cats." "That, my love," Honey said, mildly irritated, "is what we call *hurting your own feelings*."

"Mom, we can totally hear you out there," Belle calls. "It's fine. Just come in." They're lying in bed with Thumper and Jelly, clothed. Belle is holding a package of the cats' treats, reading aloud from it. "Okay," she says to me. "If you had to eat one, which would you pick? Your choices are Cheese Louise, Meat Lover, Shrimptastic, Bacon No Fakin', or Tuna Luau, which is the flavor of cultural appropriation, so don't pick that one."

"Cheese Louise," I say. "Definitely. But I want it to taste like Cheez-Its, not, like, bone meal or bull dick or whatever it actually is."

"Odds you eat one," Scriv says, and I say, "Ten to one?" and they both laugh because, it seems, that's the wrong answer to a different question.

Scriv picks Cheese Louise, and Belle picks Bacon No Fakin', since she sometimes misses bacon, and isn't planning to eat a cat treat anyway.

Jelly and Thumper are winding around the kids' arms, purring so loudly I can hear them from the doorway. "Oh my god," Scriv says. "Listen. Thumper is making his little dolphin sounds!"

"I love those sounds! Do you ever wonder if the actual dolphins just make them to annoy each other?" Belle says. "Like the way siblings do? Not even to communicate—just to be an asshole. And all the other dolphins are like, *Oh my god, stop making that stupid creaking sound before I kill you!*" When the girls were little and driving each other nuts with some or other noise, like sucking air through a flappy lollipop-filled vacuum in their cheeks, we used to say, "Some sounds are only fun to *make*." I still think that in my head sometimes, like when somebody is talking too much in a meeting. I always worry I'm going to say it out loud.

Scriv and I aren't sure about the dolphins.

"Okay, okay, you bad boys," Belle says lovingly, before feeding each cat many, many treats.

"You are a spoiler of cats," I observe, and Belle tells me that the package recommends two treats per pound of body weight, so she is in fact *under*feeding them by, like, a hundred treats.

"Look at Thumper's little face scrimple up when he chews," Scriv says, and Belle says, "I know, right? It is the actual cutest thing." News reports to the contrary, teenagers today seem so much kinder and smarter and more innocent than we were at that age.

"Do you guys want to think about making some human food?" I say. "Or we could order some before the snow starts."

"Too late," Belle says, and points out the window, where heavy flakes are falling down in clumps. "Can Scriv spend the night so we don't have to worry about the storm?"

"Of course!" I say.

"Can Dad come over? He wanted us to come there, but we're here, and it would be so cozy."

"Sure!" I say, then hum a little of "Matchmaker" to make Belle laugh, which she does.

Honey arrives, and we drag our inflated tubes and sleds out to the meadow across the way, fly screaming into the blue twilight. Up and down, slogging and flying: the alternating rigor and rapture that is the rhythm of sledding. I have a memory of the winter after Honey and I split up, when he was still professing his desperation to reconcile. Jules had been showing me pictures of the cats on her phone, only wait—"What are these?" I'd said. "Oh," she said, a little abashed.

111

"Those are from when we went sledding with Dad." And there was Honey—can't-live-another-day-without-you Honey—snow flying up around him, his head thrown back in absolute, uncomplicated joy. "Dad looks happy," I said evenly, and Jules said, "Well, Mama. I mean, he was *sledding*."

Home again now, we rub our hair with towels and change into soft clothing, make and eat a good, simple dinner of spaghetti with some of the pesto Belle froze last summer. The school texts that, given the forecast, tomorrow will be a snow day, and the kids are so happy they skip around, cheering, holding hands and ring-around-the-rosying. They decide to stay up all night. Honey boils up maple syrup and butter, pours it over bowls of clean, fluffy snow that the kids have brought in from outside. "Oooh, are we making ice cream?" Scriv asks, and Belle explains that you don't end up eating the snow. "Watch. It just chills the syrup to turn it into maple taffy." Everyone agrees that there's pretty much not a more perfect food than this. Belle and Scriv pop corn while Honey builds a fire in the woodstove, and then we look for a movie we all want to watch. We land, inexplicably, on *Jaws*. Our house is small and warm, the cats sprawl over us on their backs, and it's all as cozy as Belle predicted. Outside our windows, the snow is pouring down, and the movie is dated and weird, but still we all scream intermittently.

The night before Honey and I were supposed to sign the purchase-and-sale agreement for this house, there'd been a massive snowstorm like this, and I worried it was a bad omen. Honey listened to me fret, but my skittishness about home buying was starting to tax his patience. It didn't help that I was afraid of our agent, with her gleaming silver convertible and her preternaturally white teeth. Her facial expressions were determined by her eyebrows, which she appeared to pencil in according to the occasion: Some days they were narrow brown arches of incredulity; other days they expressed the aspirational cahoots we were all in. She'd sweep her hand in an arc near the bedroom door and exhale: "I'm picturing a master suite . . ." The eyebrows were definitely picturing this too.

"Can't you see it?" she'd say. "Not really," we didn't say. "Knock out this linen closet," she'd say. "Get rid of this smaller bedroom, and I'm picturing a *master bath!*" *Where would we put the sheets and towels?* we didn't ask. *Where would we put the children?* "I'm picturing painted beadboard," she whispered conspiratorially. "I'm picturing . . ." *Sliders. Sconces. Pocket doors. A tiled backsplash.* ("Backsplash doesn't mean there's a swimming pool," Honey had said uncertainly, reminding me of a guilty two-year-old Jules announcing, "Floss isn't for *eating.*") "I don't know," we said sometimes, and our agent and her eyebrows would mouth the word *resale.*

For a few months, Honey and I talked, thought, and dreamed about real estate with a feverishly abstracted mania. "Shed dormer," Honey would say tonelessly to me in the car as we passed a house that wasn't even for sale. "Mature plantings." "Goshen stone patio," I said back to him. "Partial views." We channeled our agent and also the listings we'd studied like scripture. We did this at friends' houses ("Open concept," we whispered to each other. "Period detailing."), and we did it while we were reading picture books to the children before bed. How in god's name could Ernie and Bert afford a brownstone in Park Slope? "Eat-in kitchen," Honey observed, looking over my shoulder while I repeated the book's preschool mantras about pouring your own juice, buttering your own toast. "Recessed lighting."

Our agent thought I was picky or weird, and I was both. One colonial she showed us backed up onto the fluorescently lit parking lot of a head-injury trauma center, and I imagined people staggering, disoriented, onto our back porch, collapsing on our wicker rocker with their heads thickly bandaged. At a sweet little ranch, I didn't like a splintery old tree house high up in a decrepit maple; I lay awake at night, picturing the children tumbling to their deaths, us wringing our hands: *This cursed house!* I didn't like a large Tupperware pitcher marked CAT LITTER on a kitchen counter. I didn't like the word *bulk-head*, which made me picture Shrek. Or Frankenstein. And I didn't like the expression *home for sale*—as if you got a whole life with your real estate: plates of meatloaf, a doting wife, enough wood for the fire. As if it were the house itself that would keep you safe, that would make you happy.

But we'd driven through the snow after all. We'd bought this little Cape house with its slopy ceilings and mismatched doorknobs. And my superstitions had proven wrong, at least for the most part. Yes, we had been safe and happy here, with the girls bouncing through the rooms like rubber balls. They lost all of their teeth under this roof! They lost all of their baby fat! They turned skinny and pimply and furious, and then sleek and kind and hilarious. But I lost something too—something besides my marriage—only I'm not sure I understand exactly what it was.

"What?" Honey says now, and I say, "What?"

He smiles. "You sighed."

I laugh, shrug. On-screen, the beaches of Martha's Vineyard are besieged by a great white shark and also pleated shorts and toxic masculinity. The wind whips snow against our windows, howls occasionally to be dramatic. The cats are snoring softly. The logs burn and shift in the stove. Belle and Scriv have braided their legs together, their faces shining in the TV light. "Nothing," I say, and smile back at him. "I don't know."

I look at my phone and there's a text from Edi. "Probably too snowy to come over tonight?" she has written, hours ago. *Fuck*. I picture a bumper sticker that says, *There are no snow days in hospice!* "I'm sorry!" I text her. "Ugh. I don't know how it got so late. I could snow-shoe over!" "It's really okay," she writes. "I'm good. I love you."

"I love you too," I write, and I squeeze my eyes shut to picture her face, paint hearts on her cheeks, sprinkle her with glitter.

"I think I might not know the difference between praying and decorating a cupcake," I say to Honey, and he laughs and puts an arm around me so that I can watch in guilty comfort as a massive prehistoric marine predator bites off everybody's legs and bodies and then gets blown to smithereens.

CHAPTER 17

Edi has lots of framed pictures on her dresser here. They're mostly of Dash. Some are of her, Dash, and Jude; others of her and Jonah and their parents before their mom died. There's one of her Brooklyn friends and another of her and Alice, both of which make me crushingly jealous. Two are of Edi and me. In one, we're four years old, sitting on a park bench, holding hands. I'm wearing bell-bottomed jeans and a jacket with a shaggy snorkel hood. She's wearing red-and-white-checked pants and a plush red coat that I coveted. She looks like a miniature fashion model; I look like a child extra from the set of *Jesus Christ Superstar*. In the other, Edi looks tragically gorgeous and comically alarmed, standing in her white spaghetti-strap gown and white satin Mary Janes, her dark hair pulled into a perfect chignon. I am behind her with a needle and thread, in my Dansko clogs and big silver hoop earrings, stitching her into her wedding dress moments before the ceremony. The fifty or so buttons running up its back turned out not to have been properly sewn on, and they'd all fallen off in my hands as I tried to button them. "This is okay, right?" she kept saying, and I kept saying back, from behind her, "This is completely fine! This is perfect." "*This* is why I'm marrying you," she said, and the photographer laughed.

"Can you help me?" Edi says from bed.

"You're awake!" I say. "Of course." She wants me to wedge a pillow under her knees to see if that will take the pressure off her hips, which are killing her. (*Killing* her!) Her legs are so swollen with fluids, so heavy and unbendingly kneeless, they're like actual logs. Logs with fuzzy SpongeBob SquarePants slipper-socks. I don't groan as I hoist them. "Like this?" I say, and she shakes her head. I move the pillows a little this way and that, and she sighs.

"I don't know," she says. "Maybe put something behind my back?"

Dr. Soprano has explained to me that some of this pain—which Edi experiences as pain in her joints—is actually being sent over by her organs as they falter. He described the liver as a kind of ventriloquist that speaks its suffering from nearby limbs and bones.

"Do you want to click your clicker?" I say. They've put Edi on a morphine pump. The brand name of the device is—I'm not kidding you—Harbinger. "I can just click this whenever I want to?" she'd asked Dr. Soprano, and he'd shrugged, nodded. "It won't let you OD, though, if that's what you're asking." "But otherwise? I just, like, go for it?"

When our old cat Brisket was dying—on the day the vet was coming over to euthanize him—I'd broiled him a whole chicken leg, which was the thing he probably most craved in all the world. After I put it out on a plate for him and lovingly encouraged him rather than swatting him off the table, he nibbled at it, excited, but then stopped and looked at me warily, like *This does not bode well*. (It did not.) The opiate smorgasbord has made Edi similarly skeptical. "I did always want to try heroin," she said, "but it just feels kind of troubling this way, like, *Help yourself!*"

It's also not clear if the drugs are really working all that well. Maybe they're diluting themselves because she's so bloated? Or maybe Edi's tolerance has become astronomically high. "Oh my god," Jonah whispered to me, the last time he was here and the nurses were upping her dosage and then upping it again. "She's Keith Richards."

Now she wants to work a little bit on the letter she's leaving for Dash, which is a combination of memories from his childhood and advice for his future self. I sit up in bed next to her, transcribe while she talks. She says a mix of normal things and crazy things: He should always splurge on Valrhona chocolate for baking, even though it costs a fortune (Okay!); he's going to feel like he'll never get over his first heartbreak, but he will, she promises him, he will feel better and better until there's just a tiny invisible scar where his heart healed (So true!); if he ever feels strange and isn't sure why, he should try eating a snack with a lot of protein in it, like cottage cheese or low-sodium beef jerky (Solid.); Bon Ami works as well as the toxic bathroom cleaning stuff and it's just made of . . . chicken bones, she thinks, or maybe eggshells? (Sounds good.); he should play tennis—he should be sure to learn tennis and play it a lot and get really really good at tennis.

I stop typing. "Hey, Eds," I say. "This one seems a little stressful to me. Nobody in your family actually plays tennis." I picture Dash with a little Björn Borg sweatband around his head, sobbing over a missed forehand. *It was my mother's dying wish!*

"Hm." She pops open a grapefruit Sanpellegrino, pours the entire can into her glass, sucks it up through a straw until it's gone, slurps around in the ice for a while. "Leave it in. Tennis just seems so *fun!*" Okay! I put square brackets around this advice to remind myself to take it out later.

He should go to an Ivy League school (this one gets the square-bracket treatment), but he doesn't have to (well, sure). "If top-notch skills are what you're after, come see us!" Edi says, a little slurringly.

It's a line from the old Technical Career Institute commercial, which ran at least thirty-seven trillion times while we were lying on Edi's floor on our stomachs, watching *Gilligan's Island* reruns and *Welcome Back, Kotter*, laughing Fiddle Faddle onto the carpet. We find the commercial on YouTube and watch it, then we watch all the old commercials for all the ice cream cakes we remember (Fudgie the Whale! Cookie Puss! Wicky the Witch!). *I am such an asshole*, is what I'm thinking. What if this is Edi's last day on earth, and she spends it listening to Tom Carvel's voice catalogue the merits of the Icy Wicy? What else is there to do, though? I mean, there's still time—not much, it's true, but how should we pass what's left?

Speaking of passing it (ha ha ha), Olga comes in to discuss Edi's bowels and their absence of movement. "Could be no poop in there," she concludes, tapping Edi's belly like it's a naughty child. "It's o-*khay*."

Edi wants to check the live feed of a pregnant giraffe she's been watching. "Oh my god! Fuck!" she says, checking the zoo website. "She had her baby and I missed it!" I ask her if she wants to watch the birth now, even though it won't be live, and she says, "Fine," and clicks the play arrow.

And it is the most astonishing thing. The female is pacing and groaning, her knees knobbed, her coat a shiny brown mosaic. The male is pacing too, and they come together, part again, come back together gracefully, like it's all been choreographed for them. Meanwhile, in the chat feed, the humans are awkward and strange. "I think it's really going to have it!" someone writes. Another person is going to go and make a sandwich—this is taking too long. "STOP WRITING IN ALL CAPS!" one agitated viewer admonishes another. And someone else writes, "I hope it dies, jk." Meanwhile, the female is straining now, grunting. She's facing the corner of her stall, and you can see something dark emerging between her legs, receding, reemerging. Her tail swishes. There it is again! It's the head! No, it's the hooves. It's the head and the hooves both, the baby folded in half maybe, the amniotic sac tearing away. And then a pause. The baby, half-born, blinks its enormous cow eyes. This creature is alive in two worlds at once, knowing them both, the before and after. Not yet here and also here. With a giant splash of fluid and limbs, the baby is falling to the floor of the stall as the mother gives a final heroic push and then turns to greet her leggy, wriggling child. Life! How on earth? I am dabbing at my eyes with my sleeve.

"Yuck," Edi says, snapping her laptop closed. "Gross."

"What did I miss?" It's Dr. Soprano in the doorway, followed by Farrah, who barges in behind him and grins at us.

"Not much," Edi says. "My eyes are closing maybe," she adds after the fact.

"Can I talk to you, Ash?" he says to me, and I say, "I'm actually just getting ready to leave."

"Take your time," he says. "Just come and find me in my office."

A little while later I'm lying on my back on his wool carpet, naked except for my wool socks. "Do what you want to me," I say. "Fuck me. I'm into it, I swear. I'm just so tired, though. I might just kind of lie here."

Dr. Soprano's cock reminds me of the zucchini my mother refers to as "baseball bats"—the kind that grow so suddenly, surprisingly large that you find them draining in the sink in a colander, shredded on the box grater and earmarked for zucchini bread because they're too big to slice and sauté. This is not a bad thing, but it might be making me feel a little extra exhausted in this particular moment.

"Hm," he says, and props himself up on an elbow, smiles not unkindly. "This doesn't feel *great* to me? Like, as a sexual encounter between willing, excited adults."

"Ugh, I know," I say. "Diagnose me."

He thinks. "Sexual narcolepsy?"

"Oh my god, is that an actual thing?" I say, and he laughs, says, "It seems to be."

I will myself to sit up, to kneel, to stretch and speak and just generally involve myself more rigorously in the *verbs* portion of this interaction. I even take my socks off. I enjoy myself surprisingly much.

"I think you might be the kindest smoking-hot person I've ever met," Dr. Soprano says to me later, looking at me in a way you might describe as *gazingly*.

"Oh god!" I say. I'm twisting my arms around to check out the rug burns on my elbows. "That makes me feel like a hologram in an episode of *Scooby-Doo*. I'm really not. I promise you."

"How you are with Edi," he says, and I say, "Please. Like, how I want to be so heroic? But then I have to force myself to come here sometimes because I'd really rather be in bed with my cats and my kid, drinking wine from the bottle and eating nachos, and already thinking about making more nachos after I finish the ones I'm still eating? You have no idea."

I'm gathering up my clothes now, putting on one item at a time and then resting on the carpet in between garments. So far I have my bra back on and also the wool socks.

"It's not a crime to be challenged by this," Dr. Soprano says gently, and I shake my head.

"I'm not *challenged by this*," I say. Somewhere in the house Golde is singing irritably, "Do I love you?" "I'm *a coward*. A jerk."

"No," Dr. Soprano says. "What you are is a little bit hinky."

"Is that the same as a little bit janky?" I ask from the floor.

"No," he says. "It's the same as not knowing the whole story about yourself."

Has Dr. Soprano just mansplained myself to me? I'm technically offended. But it's possible he's right.

CHAPTER 18

Honey came over earlier to look for an Allen wrench he needed at the shop. I loitered around while he rummaged in the toolbox.

"Do you think I'm a jerk?" I said to him, and he laughed, said, "Context?"

"No particular context."

"Then yes."

"Thank you!" I said sincerely, and he grinned at me, said, "No problem."

Now I'm back at Shapely to help Edi get ready for bed. "Can I ask you something?" she says, as minty-breathed and nightgowned as the bedtime girls when they were little. It's all I can do not to tip her face up to me so I can wipe it with a warm washcloth.

"Of course," I say.

"Are you sleeping with Dr. Soprano?"

"Oh," I say. "Gosh. Yeah? I mean, I *have* slept with him."

Edi shakes her head, says, "Ash."

"Are you judging me?" I say, and she says, "Judging you?" Her eyes flash. She seems unusually lucid, as if her whole sparkling self has reentered the building. *Incandescent*. "Am I judging you for sleeping with my hospice physician? When you have this perfect life you're just . . . *pissing* on? Yes. Yes, I am judging you."

I don't say anything.

"You attract all these people with terrible boundaries," she says. "And you just kind of hoard them all. But Honey loves you so much. Yeah, he's not perfect"—I stop myself from interjecting *Pobody's nerfect!*—"but he's a good person, good company, a great father. He's funny and handsome and loyal." This is all true. Honey's the kind of person who picks you up from the hospice where your best friend is dying, buys you a cup of coffee, and listens while you share your feelings, even if his eyebrows are raised the whole time in baffled alarm.

"And he adores you."

"I know," I say.

"That's all I want, Ash. Just to love and be loved." She's crying now. I'm crying too. "My imperfect marriage. My family. My life—to keep it. I'm sorry. I know this is guilt trippy. But what I'm losing? You're *choosing* to give it up."

"I'm so sorry, Edi," I say. I'm sitting on the edge of her bed now, holding her hands. "But also, it's not that simple."

Honey and I once rented a house on Cape Cod, and my parents came out for a couple of days. We took them to a fancy seafood restaurant at the wharf where we sat at a table over the sea, eating stuffed clams and lobster bisque, the sky the unbelievable blue of a child's painting, while a seagull stood in the window the whole entire time, choking on a starfish, hopping around on one foot, intermittently gagging and barfing, three of the starfish's five legs jutting from its mouth inches from our plates. "This is lovely," my mother said, unironically, and

I think I laughed. Absolute perfection with a gagging seagull in the middle of it sometimes feels like my entire life.

"Isn't it, though?" Edi says. "I mean, couldn't you decide that it really *was* that simple?"

Could I? I wondered as I drove home.

Marriage confused me. Some days it seemed to be just an endless sequence of body functions: the fan turned on in the smelly bathroom; the sound of someone clipping their toenails into the trash can; a waxy Q-tip on the counter; a scrim of shaved-off hairs around the sink. Another person's waste sloughing off incessantly! It can really drain a person of the will to live.

And our sex life. It was like an overgrown houseplant: rangy and neglected, straining toward the windows, some of the leaves yellowing, dropping off. But then one day it would be suddenly lush and healthy, unblighted and covered in blooms.

Sometimes, when we watched TV, Honey's palm on my thigh felt like a slice of lunch meat, just kind of *draped* there. Meanwhile, weird, dirty fragments of my time with Luca would flit past: the heavy metallic thud of a belt buckle hitting the floor; loose threads where a shirt's button had been; a damp smell like tree pollen. Luca was passionate—filthy and unreliable—and I wanted to pick and choose, to Frankenstein together some monstrous array of qualities that could never actually exist in a single person who didn't have visible bolts in their neck.

In the last days before Honey moved out, we fought. We fought late into the night, and I'd be furious that Honey was falling asleep, only I'd be falling asleep too. And I'd inadvertently battened down my hatches. I meant to say how I was really feeling—there was so much warmth inside me, so much love still—but nothing could get out. Instead, I'd become a robot set to *hyperbolic shrew*: "You never," I said. "You always." "I would be less lonely if I lived alone," I said, and I said, "That's total *bullshit*." I remember thinking that fighting with Honey was like fighting with a tub of cream cheese: There wasn't a ton of resistance, but then somehow you couldn't get out again. Around the time I was thinking this, Honey said out loud: "I feel like I'm trying to love a scalpel."

I knew what he meant. But really I was like a tragic squid, sending out clouds of poisonous ink and crying, *Why won't you see me? Why can't you find me?*

For long stretches we lay silent, waiting, fighting, fighting sleep. *Reach out your hand*, I would tell myself. But it would have taken some kind of winch to move me closer. It would have taken an earthquake. Going to bed mad—we knew it was a death knell, and we did it anyway. By the time Honey left, we were never not fighting.

But now I don't know. My handsome, hunky Honey. He was a chef when I met him, in the restaurant where I was waiting tables just after college. It was a beautiful place with ochre walls, amber-colored light fixtures, and a squat bunch of pink roses on each table. Honey made darkly delicious beef stew and perfect steak frites. He made polenta with green peppercorns and Parmesan, and bread soup glistening with good olive oil. I wore crisp white shirts and long black skirts, offered strong opinions about the food ("The duck confit. Definitely."), and made enormous tips. I flirted at the pass, thrilled to hear Honey's voice call out my orders. When he started walking me home after our closing shifts, my whole self felt buzzed up with longing, but also, paradoxically, calm. It makes no sense, even now.

Is Edi right about us? Or is this a misguided dying wish that's really not about me at all, and the next thing you know she'll suggest I train to become an Olympic pole vaulter?

"Ash?" Honey is standing in front of the couch where I'm sitting, like I've manifested him. "Sorry to startle you. I knocked as I was coming in." He sits down next to me, and my heart beats strangely. "I brought the Allen wrench back."

"Thank god," I say. "I was just getting ready to . . . Allen wrench some things." He laughs.

Belle is out with her friends, and Honey asks about her, wonders what's new. "Just that she thinks Cream of Wheat is, and I quote, *so fucking pointless*." He laughs again.

"Are you stoned?" I ask.

He puts his finger and thumb close together. "Barely."

I can smell his good smell, like pine sap and like his own warm skin. It's so familiar, this kind of humming energy between us, like a molecular disturbance. When the girls were little, we had a Fisher-Price farm that was their very favorite. They played with it all the time, bedding down the pig and cow and chicken and horse, and then rousing everybody again, filling the silo with real popcorn kernels and oats. When Honey and I wanted time alone, we'd put the batteries in, and the girls would clap and cheer: With the addition of power, the stable neighed and various things spun around and I don't even know what all else it did because I was too busy riding their dad. Honey and I referred to it as "the sex farm," and it was pretty much the favorite toy of our entire household. When I go down to get our laundry out of the dryer and see it on the basement shelf, I still flush with want. *Honey.*

Now I take his hand. "Honey," I say. "Come to bed with me."

I should be relieved that he neither recoils nor references the likelihood of getting chlamydia from my sheets, or crabs. But what he does is almost worse. He kisses me on the forehead and says, "I don't think that's such a great idea."

CHAPTER 19

Belle is lying in my bed, eating nachos and leafing through the new American Girl catalogue. "I still want all these things," Belle says, about the hippie camper and the shave-ice stand, with all their many colorful parts and accessories. "I don't even think it's just nostalgic wanting. I think it's actual *wanty* wanting." She has spent many quality hours of her life with this publication. "Actual light-up twinkle lights?" She sighs.

"Oh, shit!" She's looking close at something. "No. False alarm. I thought they finally had a butch doll, but I think it's just a boring actual boy. *Logan*. See?" I see.

She tosses the catalogue onto the floor in indignation. "You know bats?" she says.

"Yeah."

"How a bat is like a tiny little mouse—like, the smallest, sweetest thing ever? Only then it spreads its wings and it's suddenly huge and horror-movie scary?"

"Yeah," I say.

"I feel like human dicks are like that."

"Wait," I say. "What?"

Belle digs out a very loaded chip, shoves it into her mouth, tries to talk through it, then holds up a finger until she finishes chewing and swallowing. "A penis," she clarifies. "It's just soft and small, like a little innocent baby sea creature. And then it suddenly turns into this terrifying thing that's basically, like, a giant alien squid tentacle."

"Sweetie, where are you seeing so many human dicks?" I say, and she says, "Straight porn."

"Do you want to, maybe, watch *less* straight porn?" I say.

"Totally. I actually want to watch not *any* straight porn." Belle is scraping the last bits of melted cheese off the plate with her thumbnail. "Scriv and I were just curious about what straight people even *do* together. But it was much grosser than we'd imagined."

"Are there any sex things you want to talk about?" I say. Throughout elementary school, Edi and I were lectured about power-tool safety and best practices by Mr. Sumner, our shop teacher, who was missing three fingers from one hand and a thumb from the other. I have become the sex-ed version of Mr. Sumner.

"Nah," she says, "though I would totally talk to you if there were." She chews thoughtfully. "Related question, though: a crotchless thong. What does it have to offer, like, as a piece of clothing?" I can't begin to guess.

"Weren't you sexually assaulted by some guy in an underpants store? I overheard you and Dad talking about it once."

"No. I mean, maybe? I don't really know. It wasn't an underpants store—it was the lingerie department of the store where Grandma used to take me to buy bras. And the guy who worked there just, kind of, felt me up a lot. His hands were very damp and sandpapery. He would come into the dressing room when I was alone. I guess it was kind of gross, actually. But it wasn't a big deal."

Belle looks at me, skeptical and grimacing. "Yes," she says. "That is *kind of gross, actually*. I'm sorry, Mom. That's totally horrendous that that happened to you. Didn't he, like, bounce you around in his lap?"

I shake my head. "No, no. That was the hardware store guy."

"Those were the days!" Belle says. "Jaysus. Oh, also? Unrelated, but we're out of Kringle."

Kringle is a Danish cherry-filled pastry that I sometimes buy for a treat. "We're not *out of* Kringle," I say. "It's not like milk or eggs. We only have it occasionally."

"Well, can we change that?" Belle asks. "Can we just commit to having Kringle all the time? Life's too short to not have Kringle. That can be my senior quote." I laugh and say I'll think about it.

"Would it be wrong to have the cats' arms and legs removed?" Belle says. "I just want them to be more"—she pauses to put the plate down and pull Jelly up into her neck—"*beanbaggy*. They're so annoyingly opinionated about coming and going." I imagine this would be a tough sell to the vet.

"Do you know there's a *Senate upholsterer*?" Belle asks next.

I'm reminded of her toddler self, firing off random questions through the night. You'd wake to her milkshakey breath in your face: *Why a onion gots such a papery skin?*

"Like, that's someone's actual job title," she says now. Jelly is still purring into her face, despite being in full possession of all of his locomotive limbs. "Do you think that person watches congressional hearings on TV and sees something happen—like somebody's pen leaks onto their chair—and they're like, *shit*? Or are they like, *Yay! I get to reupholster that one!*? I can see it either way."

"Hey, Belle," I say.

"Yeah?"

"Does Daddy have a girlfriend?"

She looks up at me over the cat's head. "Oh," she says. "Yeah. I think he might."

"He *might*?" I say, and she says, "I guess I think he *does*, yeah."

"Do you know who it is?" I say, and she says, "It's a client of his."

"Oh my god!" I say. "*Client?* Belle, your dad's a drug dealer. *Client*." I snort.

"Geez, Mom! I meant from when he was catering, but chill, okay? And also? The people who come to Daddy's shop? They are actually called *clients*."

"Yes. Okay. Sorry." This is making Belle uncomfortable, of course. I can see that. I'm not going to ask her any more questions.

"What's her name?" I ask. "Do you know her? Do I?"

"It's Gemma," Belle says.

"The mother of the twins?" I say.

"Yup."

"The twins *Finola* and *Phineas*? Kill me." Gemma and I have been in various yoga classes together. She's pretty and English and younger than me by about ten years, which isn't as bad as it could be. I wish she were a *Desperate Housewives* type—all water-balloon boobs and gossip and abiding love for her children's ADHD medication—but she's not. She's super wholesome. She probably makes her own kombucha! Okay, that's a bad example. I actually make my own kombucha. I mean, this is the kind of town where you run into your orthodontist and his wife at *The Vagina Monologues*, for god's sake. But she's very *Irish fisherman's sweater*, Gemma is. Very *blond braid down her back*. I think that, by accident, I may have said all of this out loud.

"Mom. Stop. I'm not thrilled about it either, obviously. But you're just hurting your own feelings. You want Dad to, like, pine away for you for the rest of his life. I'm sorry, but you do. It's not right. His girlfriend's kids' names bug you, okay, whatever. I think you're going to have to get over yourself a little bit."

"You're right," I say. "You're totally right. I'm really sorry to put you in the middle."

"It's okay, Mama. I know this sucks." She passes me the cat. "You can just go ahead and feel all your feelings," she says, which is something I've said to her and Jules a thousand times. And I don't sob and say, *How on earth did I get this lucky?* I just say, "Thanks, sweetie."

CHAPTER 20

Edi has fallen. I was in the room, but asleep, and I'm still not totally sure how it happened. At some point earlier, I'd heard her crying and climbed out of bed to check on her. She was wet, and the night nursing assistant Jay helped me change her, and then she stood around shivering while Jay stripped her bed. Could she maybe just lie with me in the cot to warm up while her bed was getting remade? Jay thought that was a great idea. Edi cried, and I spooned her, and she whispered, "Get me out of here." I cried too. "I want to," I whispered, and she said, "I know you do," and then was asleep. Jay had the bundle of sheets in his arms. He smiled at me, put a finger to his lips, turned the lights off, and closed the door behind him.

And then I was awake again and Edi was on the floor, blinking up at the ceiling. "Oh my god!" I knelt down by her, dizzy. I stood up and pulled the alarm. I knelt back down and pressed my forehead to the carpet to forestall blacking out. "Oh my god, Edi!" Jay ran in. He checked her all over. *Does this hurt? What about this?* "No," Edi said, and smiled shyly, confused, still on her back. "I'm okay." Jay checked her vitals—her heart rate was elevated, but everything else seemed fine—and we got her sitting up. Her PICC line had come out. "Oh dear," Edi said slowly, looking at the place on her arm where it should have been. "Oh dear, oh dear." If Winnie-the-Pooh had ever fallen to the floor trying to escape hospice and accidentally yanked out his peripheral catheter, this surely is what he would have said.

Now Edi's got a sign on her door that says FLIGHT RISK. She's also got a motion-sensor alarm rigged up to her bed. And—worse than those things—she's got blood in her gastrostomy bag. She's asleep, and I'm waiting for Dr. Soprano. Violet came in early this morning and managed to get a subcutaneous IV inserted for the pain meds, but they need a specialist to redo the PICC. Edi's head is tipped back in sleep, her mouth open, her face caved in around it. I've definitely seen people look way more *living* than this. I am watching her chest rise and fall, sitting in a chair by the window, so tired I could barf.

The door creaks open, and an elderly patient I don't know tip-toes in, rummages in a dresser drawer, and pulls on one of Edi's sweaters before Violet rushes in after her. "Are you chilly, Lois?" Violet asks gently, then mouths *Sorry!* to me and escorts her out.

"Ash!" It's Dr. Soprano, booming quietly. "You girls had a night and a half," he says.

"We did," I say. "Oh my god."

He pulls the wheelie desk chair over by me, sits. "So," he says. "A couple things of note. Blood in the bag. Internal bleeding. We're not sure where from at this point—maybe liver, kidneys, the old surgery site in her bowels—and we won't know for sure unless it becomes obvious."

"What can we do about it?" I say.

He sighs, clasps his big hands in his lap, and leans toward me. "Nothing, really. This is the hard part of palliative care, Ash. We will try to make sure she's as comfortable as possible. That means trying to get that PICC line back in so we can keep her nice and hydrated. But no. Whatever's going on—this is the course of her illness." Violet slips in quietly, followed by Farrah. She lays Edi's folded sweater on a chair and leaves again. Farrah sits in front of me, rests her chin on my knees, waggles her worried eyebrows into my face.

"But it's not," I say, stroking the dog's ears. "I mean, she fell. I should have been awake to watch her, and I wasn't. I don't mean I blame myself. I mean, I do—but that's not even what I mean." *What do I mean?* "It just seems kind of not fair, the falling. Like, that shouldn't count as part of the natural course of things."

"I hear what you're saying. But, Ash, there aren't really exemptions in hospice. Mulligans." Dr. Soprano smiles, rubs his beard stubble with his palms. "We're not trying to game the system. It's all part of the process—Edi's agitation, the restlessness. It's something we see in a lot of our patients at this stage. Flight."

Get me out of here. Here, hospice. Here, this broken body. "Probably," he says gently, "you'll want to get the people up here now who want to be up here."

I nod. "Okay," I say. This is all too stressful and cheeseless for Farrah, who stands, stretches, sneaks out on tippy-toe paws. Aside from my raggedy breathing, we sit quietly.

"None of this is your fault," Dr. Soprano says finally, and I say, "I know."

I've twisted a tissue around and around into a kind of weepy rope that's shredding damp paper particles all over my lap. "What happens now?" I say. "I mean, with Edi."

He shrugs, nods, wheels closer to hold my hands in his, even though he's now also holding my gross tissue. "Her remaining time will unfold according to some pattern we don't really know yet. She might sleep a lot, stay closed up and do the rest of her work here internally. I would guess we'll hear a little more from her, though." He smiles. "She's a bright light, as you know. A lot of *voice*, determination."

As if on cue, something beeps on Edi's IV pole—the bag is empty—and she opens her eyes. "Strawberry shortcake," she says hoarsely.

I stand up, walk to her bedside, squat down by her. "Hey, Eds," I say, and she clears her throat, says, "Or toasted almond."

"Okay," I say.

She squints at me. "The Good Humor truck is *not* here," she says, like it's an idea she's testing out.

"Alas," I say. "It's not."

"I thought I heard it," she says.

I nod. "I think that was just your meds finishing up. But a Strawberry Shortcake bar could definitely be obtained," I say.

"Okay." She's trying to lick her lips, which are peeling. I hold out a glass of water, and she sips through the straw. I find a lip balm in her bedside drawer, dab some on her, stretching my own lips to communicate *Stretch your lips so I can put this balm on them.*

Dr. Soprano says, "Well, now that you're awake, I might as well bother you some more!" He stethoscopes her, looks into her eyes, asks her to point to anything that hurts. "This?" she says, and points to her head. "No, no. That?" She points to the window. Dr. Soprano nods, says, "Maybe both of those things." He fiddles with her IV. "You look good, Edi. Let us know if you end up needing more pain relief. Ash, walk me out?"

In the hallway he shakes his head. "Let's check in later, okay? I called my vascular guy, so we'll see if we can get that PICC line back in."

"Okay," I say, and we smile at each other sadly. "Bye!" I say, bereft—*Don't leave me alone!*—and he says, "Hang in there, Ash," and walks away.

Back in the room, Edi's eyes are open, but she doesn't seem interested in talking, doesn't need anything. I leave Jude a message, then I sit and open my laptop to write an email to our people. To Jonah and their dad. Alice and a couple of Brooklyn friends. A couple of college friends. (So many other friends! But why?) Jules, Honey, and my parents. Subject heading? *Not unexpected news*, I type, and then delete. I'm worried that someone will think, even for a single second, that she's dead. *Keeping you in the loop*, I write. I try to describe what's happening here without bogging everyone down in my own guilt and weirdness. "I'm happy to help with FaceTiming, which is definitely a great option. But, and you know how much I can't bear to write this, if you want to see Edi in person, you should probably come up here soonish." I delete *soonish* and write *soon*. I delete *soon* and write *now*. I tell everyone they're welcome to stay at my house—that we've got plenty of air mattresses and sleeping bags. I hit SEND. Then I text everyone to tell them I sent an email.

"Fuck," Jude has already texted. "I think I want to come up."

"Of course," I write back. Edi shifts around, and I stand to bend over her, but she doesn't seem to want anything.

"Fuck," Jude writes again. Then the three dots. Then nothing. "But Dash," he writes, and I write, "I know." "I don't want to bring him. But I can't really leave him."

"Ugh," I text. "Jude, I'm so sorry. Do you want to swap places with me?"

"No," he writes. "Stay with her. I'll figure it out."

My parents email that they love me, ask if I want them to come up. ("It's enough for me that you're there, that you would," I write them back truthfully.) Jonah and Jules both text that they're packing up and heading out. "Sweetheart, you totally don't have to come home," I text Jules, and she texts, "I know Mom. I want to."

Cedar pokes his head in. "Hey, Edi," he says. "Hey, Ash. Can I interest you guys in some music?" Edi swings her head around to look at him and smiles. "Is that a yes?" He is a sweetheart and a pro, this kid. He pulls up a chair, asks Edi if she has any requests, and she presses a finger to her forehead, pantomimes thinking, and says, "Doily?"

"Doily," Cedar says. "Another one I don't know." Edi shakes her head. *Not doily.* "Should I just play something I know you like?" he says, and she shakes her head again, says, "Doily," smacks her own forehead, laughs.

"Oh my god, Edi," I say. "There is definitely a word on the tip of your tongue and it's *doily*." She laughs, sighs, shrugs.

"'Across the Universe'?" Cedar says, and Edi smiles. He strums a little. *Words are flowing out like endless rain into a paper cup* . . .

I close my eyes. "I'm just going to lie down for one second," I whisper, and I climb into the cot and doze to the sound of Cedar's angel-gravel voice. *Nothing's gonna change my world.* But my world is changing.

When I wake up, Cedar's gone, and Violet's here with a box in her arms. "Something came for you, Edi," she says.

"What?" Edi asks, and Violet puts the box on Edi's desk, says, "I don't know. You'll have to open it and see!"

There's a handwritten New York return address and very strong packing tape, and I end up cutting through it with the file attachment of Edi's nail clippers. I pull up the flaps, and I can see right away what it is: a pink bakery box tied with red-and-white string. This requires fanfare! I call Jude, and when he answers, I ask if I can FaceTime him. "It's nothing bad," I say quickly, and he says of course.

We get Jude's face on the phone, and I bring it over to Edi, who waves to her husband. "Hold this," I say, and give her the phone, then I bring the pink box over. Edi looks at it, and Jude is looking too. There are two labels on the box. A small flower-shaped one in the corner says, in cursive font, LOVE, DAISY. And the other says, yes, SICILIAN LEMON POLENTA POUND CAKE. Edi smiles, raises her eyebrows.

"Oh my god!" Jude says.

"Right?" I say.

I dart out to the kitchen to grab a knife and some little plates and hurry back out, then remember the champagne—it's in the fridge, marked with a piece of masking tape that says EDI'S CAKE—and run back in for it. Back again in Edi's room with glasses and plates and silverware and the bottle, I can hear Jude talking softly to Edi, see her nodding. I lift the lid and cut into the fragrant, sugar-dotted loaf, pull out a center slice, lay it on a plate, and hand the plate to Edi. I take the phone and angle it so Jude can watch. Jude sings the *Rocky* theme song. Edi lifts the cake to her mouth, bites into it, chews, closes her eyes.

"Perfection!" Jude narrates through the phone. "The eagle has landed!"

Edi swallows, opens her eyes. "Eh," she says. She puts the plate down in her lap. "It could use a lemon drizzle or something."

I look at Jude, and he laughs. I don't have a way to tell him that, at the very least, this is the most sense she's made all day.

"But is it as good as you remembered?" Jude asks, and, bless her, Edi laughs.

CHAPTER 21

Jonah arrives, and there is much weepy, clutchy hugging in the hallway before he slips in to greet Edi, who is asleep. I promise to return soon, but I want to shower, check on the cats, be there when Belle gets home from school. I stop at the store to run in and buy a Kringle, and when I get back to my car there's a note on my windshield: *Learn to park asshole.* And then my phone rings.

It's Belle. "What's up, sweetie?" I say, and there's a pause, and a man's voice says, "Um, is this the mother of Isabelle Feld?"

"It is." *Oh my god.*

"Mrs. Feld, your daughter has been in an accident . . ." Do we all know what this means because of the TV shows we've watched? Is that why people know to say this kind of thing in the first place? Whoever this is—did he learn this line from, like, *ER* or *Grey's Anatomy?* I can hear the violin start sawing away, feel my life draining out through my feet, feel that I might be blacking out.

Only before I can finish having a heart attack and dying there in the car with a final chastising note in my hands, I hear Belle's voice—Belle's voice!—saying, "Give me the phone. She's going to have a total heart attack."

"Mom!"

"Oh my god, Belle! Are you okay? What's going on?"

"Mom, I'm fine. I think I'm fine. I'm at least mostly fine. Scriv crashed their car a little bit. They're fine too."

"Belly," I say. "Bellini." I feel the goose bumps rise all up and down my arms, feel my hair prickle off my scalp.

"I know, Mama. I'm really sorry."

"Don't be," I say. "I'm so glad you're okay. But oh my god, Belle."

"Can you come get us? We're in the ER."

I can! I do. I leave a message for Honey. I call Jonah, text Edi, although I'm not sure she's been looking at her phone. I park *like an asshole* in the hospital parking lot, rush inside. And there behind curtain number one, the game-show prize of prizes, is Belle, with a strip of gauze wrapped around her head like a cartoon character who's been in a car accident and also is a baby butch.

"Oh my god, Belle!"

"It's totally fine, Mom. It's not even a thing. There's, like, a microscopic nano-scrape on my forehead."

She lets me pull her close and kiss her, which is itself completely heartbreaking—the letting. But I just want to feel her bones under my hands, her body. I want to feel her strong, capable heart beating against my chest. I hold her face, look into her eyes, which are deep brown wells filled with my own incredible luck. I cry the very smallest amount, and Belle's own eyes fill but don't spill over.

Scriv's mom has actually already picked them up, so it's just the two of us driving home in the car. The ER doc has suggested that Belle might have a mild concussion—that I should keep an eye on her, that she should probably stay home from school for a day or two. ("That shouldn't be a problem," I say archly, and Belle rolls her eyes.) Belle asks about Edi, and I update her quickly. She tells me a little about the accident—the stereo's volume knob and a telephone pole are featured—which, even I have to acknowledge, does not sound too terrible, given that the kids' airbags didn't deploy. Belle admits that her head injury may have something to do with trying to tweeze a stray eyebrow hair in the sideview mirror. "You could have lost an eye," I say, and she says, "I just won the bet I made with Scriv about how long it would take you to say that."

"Belle," I say. I sigh. "I don't know what to think, about what's going on with you. Why you're even out driving around in the middle of a school day. I'm worried it's about your dad and me. Or about me being so messed up. And gone so much. I know it's a lot."

"Mom, I don't mean to be a jerk, but this actually isn't about you. And there's not even really a *this*, anyway. Yeah, I'm not doing every perfect thing. But I think it's just, you know, *being a teenager*. I don't think it means anything in particular." I nod. I'm driving slowly with that devastated precious-cargo feeling I had when the girls were small.

"I'm sorry," I say. "I was already feeling so sorry for myself, but then that call came from the hospital, and now I feel like I should have, I don't know, saved a little more self-pity for later."

"Feeling sorry for yourself is not a pie," Belle says gently, misquoting my favorite Amy Bloom story—"*Love* Is Not a Pie." "There's plenty of it to go around, so you can just totally help yourself."

"Thank you," I say.

"Oh my god, Mom. Did someone leave you this?" Belle is laughing suddenly. "You are having the *worst* day! I'm taking a picture of this. *Learn to park asshole* on a Life Is Good Post-it note?"

"I know, right?" I say. I'm laughing too.

"Wow," she says. "We should have known this year was going to be shit when we had that interfaith disaster."

Just before New Year's, our menorah caught the thatched roof of our creche on fire, and before we were able to douse it, our curtains were singed, the chimney was burnt off our gingerbread house, and a nearby bowlful of gelt was partially melted.

"Look behind you, though," I say, and she does, and there's Kringle on the back seat. "You're the actual best," she says, and I know she at least mostly means it.

CHAPTER 22

Jules is there when we get home, and Honey is too, and we all hug each other and laugh and cry, with the cats winding around our legs. (This is the configuration of children and pets that Honey calls the Boys and Girls Club.) I wrap my arms around Jules; Honey inspects Belle's head; Belle lifts Jules off the ground. I whisper *Sorry I hit on you* to Honey, who laughs and shakes his head.

"Mama, I want to go see Edi," Jules says. "But also I'm just really scared about seeing her."

"I know, pussycat," I say. "I feel like that too. That's totally how it is right now. Do you want to go and just plan on staying for a bit?" She does. Honey is going to stay home and keep an eye on Belle, who seems, I have to admit, perfectly fine. "Do you have homework?" I ask her, and she says, "Yeah, World Lit, but I'm not supposed to read because of maybe having a concussion. Which, yay, because Odysseus is such a fucking narcissist that I can't even deal with that shit anymore." Honey raises his eyebrows at me, and I laugh. "Daddy, can you just roll me up in a blanket and rock me like a tired burrito baby?" she asks, and, yes, this can be arranged.

On the way to Shapely, I try to warn Jules about the way Edi looks.

I don't want to be dramatic about it, but it's also very surprising to see her now—her gray skin and deep eye sockets, her swollen legs, her large teeth and thin lips. I don't tell her about Edi's mustache, which is growing in a little, and which I don't know what to do about, since she hasn't mentioned it. What if she died while I was tweezering out her mustache hairs? This seems not completely out of the question. "Just, like, it's not hard to imagine that she's dying," I conclude. "I don't want you to be shocked."

"Okay," Jules says uncertainly.

There's a mortuary van pulling out of the Shapely parking lot as we arrive. "Oh no!" I say, and Jules says, "What?"

"I don't know."

But as soon as we see the votive candle burning in front of his room, I do. It's Junior. "I didn't even realize he was sick!" I say, and Jules says, "Um, Mom?" Because *hospice*. But still. I close my eyes just for a second, picture Junior's merry face, kiss his pale, wrinkly cheeks, sprinkle him with stardust.

Edi's eyes are open when we walk in, but it's not clear if she sees us. Jonah shrugs, smiles, stands up to embrace Jules, to embrace me. "It's okay," he says to Jules, who's hesitating. "She'll be so glad you're here."

"Hey, Edi," Jules says, squatting down by the bed, and Edi turns her head, smiles down at her.

"Wow!" Edi says. "Indigo?" she asks, and Jules says brightly, "Probably!"

Edi shakes her head. *Not indigo.* "Your mom's friend is sick," she says, tentatively.

"Yeah," Jules says.

"How is she?" Edi says. She's got a glass in her hands, and she keeps shaking it so that the ice rattles, water sloshing out. She passes Jules a washcloth, and Jules mops up Edi's lap, her own coat.

"Okay, I guess," Jules says. "I don't know. Not great."

Edi smiles at Jules, nods sympathetically, then sees me, gestures for me to come over. I bend down to her, and she whispers, "Is Dash here?"

I shake my head. "He's not," I say, and she says, "Thank god," and flops backward onto the pillows, closes her eyes, seems to be immediately asleep.

"Wowza," Jonah says quietly to Jules, and she says quietly back, "Oof."

A moment later, the door cracks open and Jules says, "Oh my gosh! Miss Norman?" *Kill me!*

"Hey, Jules! Hi, everybody," she says to us. "Just checking in to see if you guys need anything."

"What I need is for Ruth to turn up *Fiddler on the Roof*," I say, "because I can't even hear it."

Miss Norman—Jen—presses her lips together, shakes her head. "Ruth's not feeling so hot," she says, and I say, "Seriously?"

She nods. "It happens here," she says quietly. "Lots of decline at once. February can be a rough stretch." Luckily, it's the *last day* of February! A nice, short month. Maybe we all just need to make it to March.

"Is it okay if I pop in to see her?" I say, and she says of course. I tell Jonah and Jules—and Edi—that I'll be right back, and walk down the hall to Ruth's room. Her head is tipped back on her pillow, and she's breathing slowly and noisily, like there's something in her throat. She is, inexplicably, wearing one of Edi's cardigans. A gift from Lois?

"I'll just help myself," I say quietly, and take a lemon drop from her tin. I hold her cool hand for a minute, sing a little bit of "Sunrise, Sunset," kiss her cheek.

A young woman comes in—a granddaughter, I think—and I

stand up, say, "Sorry—I was just avoiding my own dying person in the next room."

She smiles. "I know," she says. "This is so hard. I was just in the kitchen singing 'Tradition' and stress-eating chocolate-chip mini muffins." I hug her and tell her how amazing Ruth is, and we wish each other luck. I pull the door closed on my way out. Everywhere, behind closed doors, people are dying, and people are grieving them. It's the most basic fact about human life—tied with birth, I guess—but it's so startling too. Everyone dies, and yet it's unendurable. *There is so much love inside of us.* How do we become worthy of it? And, then, where does it go? A worldwide crescendo of grief, sustained day after day, and only one tiny note of it is mine.

In Edi's room, in my absence, the festivities have begun. Honey and Belle have arrived with takeout—"It was too lonely without everyone" is Belle's excuse for violating her stay-at-home orders—and they're unpacking cartons and containers, Thai soups and noodles perfuming Edi's room with basil, chiles, lime leaf. And then the door opens again, and it's Jude and Alice. *Hi! Hello!* Everyone embraces and cries, and Edi from her bed grins and grins at Jude, tips her face up to him to be kissed. "Hello, my beloved wife," Jude says, and kisses her. None of us can help watching them.

Alice unzips her full-length platinum puffer jacket, and she's wearing leather jeans and a snug white cashmere turtleneck. "Jesus," I say, and she says wistfully about her own glamorousness, "I know," and then, "I promise it'll be less fancy when it's got curry all over it." Alice is that annoying mix of gorgeous and wealthy and entirely down-to-earth. You want to begrudge her everything, but you can't even begrudge her one single thing because she's so funny and generous. She did my hair and makeup at Edi's wedding, and I had never looked more effortlessly stunning in my life; if the roles had been reversed, I probably would have on-purpose painted her up like a rouged gargoyle. She is unbearable, and I love her against my will.

"Is it weird that I'm still jealous of Alice?" I say quietly to Jude. "The way Edi looks at her—I mean, even now?"

"Oh, please," Jude says. "As you may recall, I'm the person who had a total conniption when Edi's high-school boyfriend sent her flowers at motherfucking *Sloan Kettering*. I might not be the right person to ask."

Plates are filled and passed, caps popped off beer and prosecco bottles. We are having a bona fide party! Edi's got a glass of bubbly and a chocolate pudding cup from the kitchen. We drag in a couple of extra chairs from the conference room. Farrah Fawcett joins us. Jude gets Nina Simone to pour out of somebody's speaker. Belle's got a Band-Aid on her head and maybe a concussion, but still both girls gleam almost obscenely: shiny, pink cheeks; shiny, dark hair—Jules's long and curly, Belle's short and bristly—and huge smiles. I catch Honey's eye: *We made these people.* Jude is telling Jules the cake story, and Jules is laughing her sleigh-bells laugh. Belle is asking Jonah something about his work, and I hear her say, "I know it's not actually a *hedgehog* fund? But I always *think* it's a hedgehog fund." Alice is bent over Edi, talking and laughing quietly, tears glinting like diamonds in her long eyelashes. Nina Simone is feeling good. I'm standing with a can of bitterly delicious beer in my hand, beaming and beaming—my jaw actually aches from smiling so much. I have never been so sad and happy in my entire life. The whole time Edi's been here, I've thought: *Live like you're dying? Who would do that? Dying sucks.* Now I see it, though. I *do* want to live like this! When I say this to Honey, he laughs and says, "I think you've always taken that saying a little too literally."

Eventually, Dr. Soprano pops his head in and says, "Wow—we should have given Edi the suite!"

"There's a suite?" I say, and he says, "No. I was kidding." He comes all the way into the room, introduces himself to Jules and Alice, embraces Jude. Then he loiters around, gazing at the food and drink, pad thai all but visible in a thought bubble over his head, until Jude invites him to help himself, which he happily does. Miss Norman joins us briefly too, during which time Belle catches my eye and holds up three fingers, and I scratch my cheek with my middle finger to make her laugh. "That's not even counting Dad," she sidles over to whisper, and I say, "What? I can't hear you," and push my ear toward her with my middle finger. "This is a unique situation," I say, and she whispers, *A unique hospice sausage party.*

I join Jude and Jonah, ask about Dash. He's with his grandfather—Edi and Jonah's problematic dad has come to Brooklyn—which seems less than ideal. "Is that okay?" I say, and Jude says, "Is any of this okay?" I nod. "Good point."

"And is your dad okay with not being here?" I ask Jonah, and he shrugs. "Okay enough, apparently," he says. "I know he's not your favorite person, Ash. But I feel protective of him. He really is crazy about Dash. About Edi too. And he's just coping in his own way."

"Of course," I say. "I know he must be devastated. I can only imagine." *My daughters!* I chase the thought out of my brain with a raised broom.

Still, it's true that Edi and Jonah's dad is not my favorite. He's the kind of person who pretends not to have heard of the college you're going to if it's not Ivy League—even if it's, like, down the street from him and it's NYU. Back when we were kids, all the fathers were weirdly absent, of course. They left with a briefcase every morning and did god knew what until they came home and drank scotch, chain-smoked Pall Malls, or, if they were quitting, chain-smoked reduced-tar Trues. You saw them on the weekends, when they made French toast and let you watch *60 Minutes* with them as long as the football game didn't run over. You gave them lumpy pottery ashtrays for Father's Day; I picture the kiln at our school, just filled to bursting with ashtrays that kids were making for their dads. I can hardly express to the girls how different the man I grew up with is from the one who listens attentively, nodding and scooping up hummus with pita chips, while they explain to him the concept of ableism and why he should stop saying, "A blind man could see it."

Meanwhile, Edi's mom had been beautiful and languorously busy. She'd been on various boards of directors of various art museums and libraries. We'd come home to a note, scented with her oily, expensive perfume, that listed things we could do to better ourselves in her absence: a Haydn sonata to listen to; this or that *New Yorker* article to read; perhaps we could get some exercise and work on losing a little weight. "Are we fat?" I said to Edi once, and she shrugged and said, "I really don't know." There'd be a separate note for Jonah about practicing the clarinet, reading Hannah Arendt, taking out the trash, drying out his acne. My own mom was more likely to get out her sewing machine and help us make wedding dresses for our dolls, or walk us the few blocks to the store that sold the Lip Smackers, where she sniffed each contender indulgently. My own mom let us eat cake for breakfast because what was the difference, really, between cake and a Danish?

"Not to belabor this, but your dad actually introduced himself to me at Sloan last month," I say to Jonah, and he recoils, horrified.

"He didn't!"

"Yes. He did. He walked in, stuck his hand out for shaking, and said, 'I'm Myron, Edi's father.'"

Jonah shakes his head. "Did you say, 'I'm Ash, Edi's best friend for her whole life'?"

I laugh. "Yes."

"I'm sorry," he says, and I say, "Oh god, don't be. *I'm* sorry. I really should be complaining about this to someone else. Also, he did give me twenty dollars to take a taxi home, which was nice."

"But did you take a taxi home?" Jonah asks, and I say, "Of course not. I took the subway like a normal person."

"So, basically, you profited from that exchange," he says, and I say, "That's why you're the money guy."

Everyone goes suddenly quiet because Edi has something to say. Nope! She doesn't. She was just shaking the ice in her cup, and Alice thought she'd wanted to make a toast or a speech. So we decide we'll do it instead. We take turns telling funny stories, telling her how much we love her, how enriched our lives have been by her. Alice talks about the time they went to Jamaica together. ("Um, I'm sorry, did my invitation get lost in the mail?" I whisper to Jonah, and he says, "They probably actually went to Croatia.") They bought a bag of sticky bud from some dude on the beach, only it turned out to be a popsicle stick with oregano glued to it, like a scam ganja craft project. Edi smiles, shakes her ice, tips her face up to be kissed by Alice, who cries and laughs and says, "That's such a dumb story! I meant to say you're brilliant and the best friend ever."

Jules reminisces about Edi building fairy houses in the backyard with her. "And fairy snack bars too—Chipmunks Welcome!" she adds. Jude talks about getting down on one knee on the Staten Island Ferry, asking her to marry him, Edi grimacing because, as it bizarrely turned out, her ex-boyfriend had also proposed to her on the Staten Island Ferry. ("Oh my god, Edi, and you told him that?" I said at the time, and Edi said, "Yes. My filter seemed to be malfunctioning.") "I was like, 'So no?'" Jude says. "And she was like, 'No, no, yes! Totally yes! It's just so creepy.'" Jonah tells the story about Edi taping over his haftorah, and then I panic—That was the story I was going to tell!—and instead tell this completely random story about Edi spilling an entire black currant yogurt into her purse on the Chunnel train and apologetically handing the conductor her yogurty passport while I laughed so hard I peed in my pants and then had to sit on a stolen hotel towel for the rest of the ride. "Sorry," I say. "Same as Alice said— you're also brilliant and the best friend ever. The best, best friend."

Edi is grinning at us quietly, mildly bewildered, shaking her ice, shaking her PEG tube occasionally, clearing her throat—which keeps making everyone think, all over again, that she wants to speak, and she doesn't. But she's here with us—listening, soaking it all in, I hope, gathering supplies for the hard journey ahead. Gathering love, and there's so much of it in this room. If love were helium, Shapely would lift up and away, drift off and float skyward with all of us in it. I wish that would happen. I don't know what would happen after, but that would be enough for now. Just all of us suspended.

I want to stay in the deep thrum of the profound, but I don't. Instead, I notice that Edi's nail polish is peeling—should I remove it?—and that Honey's wearing a sky-blue sweater I've never seen before, and that it looks great on him. The toasts are over, and Belle is laughing with Jonah, flashing the perfect gap between her front teeth. Jules is leaning against me, so grown-up in her tights and boots, and her hair smells like apples. Everyone is so beautiful. I'm seeing all of us surrounding Edi in this room, her bed in the middle like a raft. I'm seeing Shapely on the grid of the town's streets and buildings, seeing the town in the state, the state in the country, the country on the globe, the earth in the boundless, endless universe, surrounded by infinity, spinning pointlessly. I slip outside into the hallway to catch my breath, and Honey follows, squats down by me. "You okay?"

"Yeah. I think I'm having vertigo. Or, like, an existential crisis."

Or apeirophobia, which, Jules has explained to me, is the fear of eternity, which I am definitely having. Where will Edi *be*? And for how long? *Nowhere and forever.* No.

"I know," Honey says. "It's too much."

"It's too much," I agree.

And because it's *really* too much, Shapely snaps into action around us, nurses and nursing assistants and volunteers entering the rooms along the hallway to cheer and distract while two men arrive with a gurney and head for Ruth's room.

Honey puts an arm around my shoulder, kisses the side of my head.

"I love you," I say, and he says, "I know you do," and then—because I have pulled away to look at him, aghast—he laughs and quietly sings part of an old Maria McKee song. "Why wasn't I more grateful? When life was sweet . . ." "You are secretly a dick, and I'm the only person in the world who knows it," I say, but I'm laughing, and he says, "I know. I love you too."

CHAPTER 23

Jude is staying with Edi tonight, so the rest of us are back at the house. One thing I've started to suspect about myself is that I'm some kind of confusingly extroverted introvert. I just want to sit here on the couch with a tumblerful of the good booze Alice brought, soak in the music and the conversation, and not talk to anyone. I want to be invisible and lie down on the couch and fall asleep to the muffled sounds of conversation, like a child in the back seat of the car being driven safely through the night by grown-ups who love her.

"Nobody mind me," I say. "I'm just lying down for a minute. Help yourself to everything." And so I curl up at one end of our pink living room couch with my head on Belle's huge plush sloth pillow, Jelly curls up into the crook of my hip, and I listen to everybody talking. Jonah is telling Belle and Honey about a conversation he'd had with Edi during the snowstorm—how she'd referred to a *power outrage*. "Power *outage*?" he'd asked, and she'd said, no, no, she could see the word in her mind, and it was definitely *outrage*, and he'd thought that it made sense in a roundabout kind of way. Jules is admiring Alice's spingly-spangly earrings—they're huge and complicated, like a fringed macrame wall hanging strung with crystals—and telling her a little about college life, about the magnetism lab where, on the first day of her internship, she'd felt the thin chain around her neck tug and then snap as it flew toward a rare-earth neodymium magnet the professor had pulled from a cupboard; "'I hope you didn't imagine this was solid gold,'" she quoted her professor saying to her, handing back the broken necklace, "'because this most certainly contains a ferromagnetic core.'"

On the other side of me, Belle is talking about the platypus farm she imagines—"You could produce milk *and* eggs!"—before checking to see if anyone wants to refresh themselves with a popsicle. "Full disclosure, though—I made them with just water, so they're very . . . *plain-tasting*." Alice requests one, and then plunks it directly into her whiskey glass.

"Do you ever get one of these," Honey is asking Belle, holding up his thumb, "this thing that's, like, a weird little flap of skin at the edge of your nail?"

"Dad, a *hangnail*?" Belle says, and he says, "No, no. Not a hangnail. Like this little flap of dry skin next to your nail, and if you pull it it either pulls off easily or it goes really deep?"

Belle shakes her head. "Dad, that's called a *hangnail*. Yes, everybody gets those."

"Really?" Honey says. "I always thought a hangnail was just when part of your nail was, like, hanging off for no reason."

"Mom, are you listening to this?" Belle says, and I laugh from the couch and say, "I actually am."

"I can't believe you've gone your whole life without knowing what a hangnail is," Belle says, "Who even are you?" And Honey shrugs cheerfully, says, "I contain multitudes."

My people are circling closer, migrating over. The coffee table is full of glasses now, of bottles empty and half-empty, of clementine peels and open bags of potato chips. Belle hoists my legs into her lap and sits without disturbing the cat. Jules is sitting on the floor by us and stroking Jelly, whom Belle is lovingly chastising, "Stop grunting! You're a bad gruntling." Jules muses about something I've heard before too, which is the way cats supposedly know when someone's dying. "They cuddle up with that person and purr, apparently, and it's one of the ways, I guess, nurses and caregivers know that death is near." We wonder about the dogs at Shapely—do people think dogs know too? Everyone agrees that Farrah Fawcett might care more about your dying self if it were dunked in queso dip.

"Only kind of related, but does anyone else feel like Dr. Soprano is weirdly hot?" Alice asks, and Belle laughs out loud, says, "Ew, no," and then looks at me and says, "I mean, he's great, though." Alice laughs too and says, "No, that's fine. I guess he really isn't your type, Belle."

Belle wonders aloud about her type, and what it is, and I say, "Is Scriv not your type?" and she says, "Scriv? Oh. God. Definitely not. I mean I love Scriv, but no." I really know nothing, it turns out.

"She likes *girls*, Mom," Jules says to me, like there's a dial tone in the place where my brain activity should be occurring. And then to Belle, "Isn't your type, like, Alicia Keys? Billie Eilish?"

"Well, sure," Belle says, and sighs. "Not super actionable, but true." Honey looks at his watch, stands up, and stretches, says he should probably head home. I drag myself to standing too and pull on somebody's snow boots so that I can walk him all the way outside. We can see our breath in the dark air, and Honey hugs me. "Thank you," I say. "It means so much to me that you're here for this. I know it's so grounding for the girls. For me too."

"It's my pleasure," he says. "I mean, not pleasure exactly. Obviously. But it's good. It feels, I don't know—like this totally distilled moment."

I nod. "That's how it feels to me too," I say.

He hugs me again, kisses my cheek. He smells like woodsmoke and oranges. I stop my hands from rubbing the stubble on his cheeks. "I'm sure I'll see you tomorrow, Ash. Text me if there's anything, okay?" I say of course I will, and he walks down the path to the street, turns and waves, walks to his car and drives away. It's clear and very cold outside. I'm just wearing—what am I wearing? The same gray sweater of Jonah's I've been wearing for days. I pull my hands up into the sleeves and tip my head back to look at the stars, the moon that's like a little sideways smile—*a toenail clipping moon* is what Belle has always called this type of crescent. There's an owl hooting from a nearby pine tree, and another owl hooting back from somewhere farther away. And there's another sound too, that's just the snow doing something—settling, with a little crackle, the way a cake does when you take it out of the oven. My walkway is shoveled. I notice this for the first time, though I've been walking on it since the storm. *Honey.*

A text dings in. It's a local friend inviting me to go ice-skating on the pond near her house. "You don't even have to talk," she texts. "Just come enjoy the ice. Not now, obvs," she adds. "Like, over the weekend." I tell her that I think we're in the homestretch with Edi (Because suddenly I'm some kind of a *baseball* expert?), and she texts a string of hearts, her love, her standing offer to help in any way. My mom and dad have written too, to ask for updates, to express their bottomless love for me. My luck wells painfully, like blood into a cut.

Every year, ever since the girls were born, I have blown out the candles on my birthday cake and wished for *just this.* Everything I have already. No loss. *I can't spare anybody* is what I always think. But, then, people must be spared. That is the whole premise of this life, of this time we have with each other.

The door opens, and it's Jonah. "Um, are you lying in the snow?" he says.

"Am I?" I say. "Oh, I am! Just for a minute. I'm just thinking, I guess. Or drunk."

"Everybody's getting ready for bed," he says. "Do you want to come inside and make out with me?"

"Oh, Jonah," I say. "I probably don't. I love you. Don't hate me."

"Oh god, of course not," he says. "Never. This is all so weird. Just come inside anyway, though. To not make out—just because it's fucking freezing out here and we miss you and you're scaring me a little bit."

Inside, Jules and Belle are in the living room blowing up air mattresses (some dickweed I was dating once corrected me when he was fixing my bike tire—"It's *inflating*, not *blowing up*"—and now I will never use the word *inflate* again), and Alice is brushing her teeth at the kitchen sink, wearing what appear to be neon pink cashmere pajamas. I insist that she take my bed, that Jonah take Belle's, and I fetch them clean bedding. I just want to camp out with the girls downstairs.

"Cats get trapped sometimes," Belle is warning Thumper, who has snuck under the fitted sheet she's trying to stretch over the air mattress. She makes up the bed around him, and he's a vibrating, excited lump, exactly the way the girls were when they were little—inserting themselves everywhere—*Don't find me! Come and find me! Here I am!*

I bank the fire in the woodstove, take off my sweater and jeans, pull my bra out from under my T-shirt, and climb into the sleeping bag I've unrolled on the couch. "Do I have to brush my teeth?" I say out loud to nobody in particular, and the girls chorus, "Definitely not!" They've moved the coffee table to push the heads of their mattresses up against the couch where I'm lying, and I doze, listening to them gossip about the cats. *Have you ever seen stripier paws than this? I seriously have never. Look at his whiskers! I know, right? They're actually so much longer and droopier than the way we've always drawn them. Smell his stinky yawn hole!* The last thing I remember hearing is Belle say, in answer to something Jules has asked, "I guess mist is probably my *third-favorite* form of precipitation?" and Jules saying, "Well, sure. I mean, after rain and snow, obviously."

Obviously.

Sleep, which has been playing a dully exhausting game of hide-and-seek with me for months, shows up out of nowhere and drags me to the bottom of the ocean floor, where I dream the deep-sea dreams of the drowned. Of the oblivious.

CHAPTER 24

I wake up to the sound of Jonah and Alice talking quietly. I can smell the coffee they've brewed in my elderly Chemex, and the part of my brain that keeps track of addictions lights up with stubborn joy.

Alice is boiling eggs. "How do I sustain injuries overnight *while I'm sleeping?*" I hear her ask Jonah, indignant. "I mean, like, I went to bed last night and now I basically have tendonitis in my wrist somehow."

"Aging." Jonah sighs. "It's not for the faint of heart."

"I guess it beats not aging," Alice says, and Jonah says, "Too true."

Jonah sees that I'm awake and—bless him—brings me a cup of hot, milky coffee. I sit up in my sleeping bag to drink it, admire the girls' faces, turned toward each other in sleep. They still look like babies this way: their thick crescents of dark eyelashes, their soft pink cheeks and red lips. Their hands are clasped above the comforter.

I hear the cats up on the kitchen counter, telling Jonah and Alice their sad story about how they starved all night. "Should I, uh, try to feed these guys?" Jonah asks, pushing Thumper back with a nervous elbow. He's not really an animal person. "No, no," I say. "I got it." I pull on my jeans, note my hangover, drink a big glass of water over the kitchen sink, and rinse the cats' bowls. They roar and chuff like miniature lions. "*Nobody* did?" I'm saying to them, pouring out their clattery food. "All night? Really? Your stomach actually digested itself? You poor, poor boys."

Alice and I swallow small handfuls of Advil while Jonah tries to read the proper dosage aloud to us from the bottle. Alice peels her eggs, asks after salt, hot sauce. Nobody has heard from Jude. We decide we'll just shower and dress and head over to Shapely. I change my underpants in lieu of anything actually involving soap and water, wrangle back into my bra, pull on Jonah's sweater, wait with my coffee for those guys to get ready.

I text Jude that we're heading over soon, and he writes back, "Great. We've got a request here. Pringles? Not 100% sure it's that but can you guys get a can?" We can! Ha ha ha. *Can*. Kill me. Alice and Jonah appear, clean and fresh and great-smelling. I lean into Alice's neck. "What is that?" I say, and she swishes her hand in the air. "Something fancy and expensive. Sandalwood. Lichen. Burnt tires. I can't remember."

"Hey, nice sweater, by the way," Jonah says, and I say, "Thank you," and dab.

I leave a note for the girls and we head out, stop for chips, and then, while we're at the market, gather a few other supplies. Grapefruit seltzer and watermelon chunks and the cold-brew coffee Edi likes to drink, even in winter. Half-and-half. Two bottles of Chianti. Passion fruit lip balm and Jolly Ranchers and peppermint hand lotion. Strawberry Shortcake bars. Toasted Almond bars. *Cosmopolitan* magazine and the *New York Times* and salami with fennel seeds and a pocket guide to astrology. We arrive at Shapely with an inexplicable number of bags, stop at the sanitizing station, approach Edi's room with something like dread.

Edi's eyes are closed. Jude's eyes are red-rimmed, his curly hair pressed flat on one side. "Oh, you poor thing," I say, and hug him. He shakes his head. "I'm okay," he says. "It was okay, the night. Not great, but okay." We take off our coats, unload the bags in the kitchen, bring the chips back in. Jude tells us about Edi waking on and off, rattling her glass, needing more and more to drink.

"Is this it?" she'd asked plaintively at one point—the only words she'd spoken—and he said something like, *I don't know, sweetheart, but I'm here, I love you, you'll go when you need to go*, and she'd cleared her throat and said, "No. Is this the last of the Pellegrinos?" and he'd said, "Oh! No. There's more. I'll grab one."

(Because, heads up, your stay in hospice will be scripted by Abbott and Costello.)

"I worried that those were going to be the last words I ever spoke to her," he's telling us, "but luckily she woke at dawn and asked if there was any more champagne, and I said, 'There's not.'" He laughs, sighs. "So maybe *those* will be the last words I ever spoke to her."

Edi's eyes are open now, and, instead of, say, telling her how much I love her, I peel the foil off the top of the Pringles can and hold it out to her. (*Raisins?*) She reaches into the chips, tentative and clumsy— her fingers are swollen now too—and then her hand is briefly stuck in the can like it's one of those grabby finger traps. But once she gets the hand back out, she bites into an entire stack of chips, crumbs spraying everywhere while we all say ridiculous, encouraging things—"Good, right?" "I mean, is there any problem a Pringle *can't* solve?"—and then she coughs. She chokes. Clearly, there's a Pringle lodged some- where along Edi's airway. She is coughing and gagging, and I run out to get someone—run into Olga in the hallway, who hurries be- hind me back into the room.

The girls and I once listened to a podcast about an astronaut in the 1960s who'd smuggled a corned-beef sandwich onto the *Gemini 3*. It was meant to be a tasty and comedic surprise for his shuttle mate—only then it all went awry, because once they hit zero gravity, the sandwich began breaking up. It hadn't been vetted by ground control or, really, anybody except maybe the deli guy, and before long the airspace was filled with crumbs of mustardy rye bread and free-floating hunks of garlicky cured meat, all of which lodged into various onboard control panels and apparatuses. There's even a transcript of the astronauts talking about it—"I've had better ideas," the sandwich bringer says, understatedly. A House representative, critiquing NASA's funding and safety record, referred to it as *the thirty-million-dollar sandwich*.

All I'm trying to say is that I'm the kind of person who would bring an unsanctioned corned-beef sandwich onto a spaceship. And also: The Pringles were a bad idea.

Olga, calm, gives Edi a single sharp smack between her shoulder blades. "You are not for lungs," she admonishes the chip after it flies out of Edi's coughing mouth. Edi coughs some more while Olga checks her IV, looks at her eyes, pulls the blanket back to look at her feet. "You made improvement," Olga tells Edi, and then, to us, on her way out, "Soft foods."

Edi is still catching her breath, drinking from a glass of something, coughing a little. "Good morning, everybody!" Jude says, and we laugh. We're rattled. It's March first.

The only sound in the room is Edi's continued drinking, the clattering of the ice in her glass, and I feel like I'm hosting a dull and stressful party. But here is Laura, the Shapely chaplain, coming to rescue us from the social awkwardness of sitting around while somebody dies. She bends down to greet Edi, introduces herself to the others, and asks us quietly if we might want to do a guided meditation with her in the conference room. We do! Well, Jonah doesn't—but that's good, because he can keep Edi company. Jude, Alice, and I follow Laura across the hall.

Once we're seated, Laura asks to us to bow our heads and then talks to us about how rare and challenging this experience is, facing the death of a loved one. She invites us to feel the fullness of our feelings, to consider what our intentions are for this time, to allow ourselves compassion for ourselves as well as Edith. "It's hard to talk about the d-word," she says, and I look up, make eye contact with Alice, who mouths quizzically, *Douche?*

And then Laura asks us to close our eyes. She uses a small mallet to bang a miniature gong. She talks to us about breath, asks us to *be with* our breath, to let our thoughts and judgments come and go. Instead, my mind races, and I race after it: *I hope Jude wants to sneak out and smoke after this*, I think. Breathing in, breathing out, *and also wondering if Edi thinks of Alice as her best friend. Sorry I didn't buy her a mohair lap blanket or whatever!* Inhale. *Wasn't there that one episode about the English vet guy where he thinks he's euthanized a sheep, only then he returns later, and the animal's fine, and the farmer thinks that maybe it just needed a good long rest? Could we, like, put Edi to sleep for a little while, to give her body time to heal itself?* Exhale. *Fuck—that probably doesn't count as* acceptance. *Popcorn shrimp*, I think, apropos of nothing. *Does Edi still have my old SAVE THE WHALES T-shirt? Would it be awkward if I asked Jude to look for it?*

I refocus. Laura is asking us to imagine the first breath we ever took. Instead, I remember the girls, right after birth, lying on my chest and looking directly at me with their filmy little no-color eyes— that crazy feeling of *somebody's home*, which even those brand-new pupils could telegraph. There's a giant, rolling bowling ball in your belly, and then, somehow, this person. This *consciousness*. Where was it before? And where does it go *after*? I've been so focused on keeping the girls alive all these years that this is the first moment that I truly understand the inevitability of their deaths, however timely they turn out to be, however—knock wood—blessedly long after my own. "Now imagine the last breath," Laura says, and I do. I already have.

"Breathe in acceptance," Laura says. "Breathe out peace." She strikes the gong again, asks us to open our eyes, gives us a minute to collect ourselves, asks if we have any questions.

I do. "Is there something—like *closure*, I guess I mean—that we should be trying to help Edi with right now?"

Laura nods, smiles at me kindly. "You're really just along for the ride at this point," she says. "You don't need to search for meaning on her behalf, for finality. Whatever Edith needs to do now is what she's doing—it's not really about you."

I nod, ashamed. "It's at least *mostly* about you, Ash," Jude says, to make me laugh.

"I don't mean that unkindly," Laura continues. She touches a kind of pale purple stalactite (stalagmite?) that's hanging at her throat. "I just mean that Edith doesn't want to die—she's not fully at peace with the idea—so she might not come to anything that feels satisfying. She might not make meaning of her life and death. She might, of course. I mean, we always hope for that because it makes us feel better. But she might not." We're all quiet for a moment. "Anybody else?" Laura asks.

Alice and Jude shake their heads.

"I have another question," I say. "Sorry. But—will the doctor be with us when she dies? Or will you? I think I don't understand how this works."

Laura nods. "It depends on what you need, to some extent. On who's around." Even as she's speaking, I realize that I'm still thinking of birth. How it's nurses and friends and partners until the last moment, when a doctor swoops in for the delivery. Are we just going to midwife Edi on our own? Are we capable of it?

"I think I'm just worried that I, like, don't have this particular skill set," I say.

"The only skill you need now is love," Laura says, "and you definitely have it." We are in a windowless space with generically upholstered chairs, talking about everything in the world that matters most.

"Sorry, Jude," I say, because I feel like I'm taking up too much space, and he puts an arm around me, says, "You're good, Ash. You're fine."

"You're at a loss," Laura says. "Literally. Try to be forgiving of yourself."

It's absurd, this conversation, and also utterly profound—like the existential version of putting nutritional yeast on popcorn. Hippie-dippie bullshit, but then it's so, so good.

"Thank you," I say to Laura. "This was super helpful." And she presses her palm flat on my sternum in a way that allows me to take an actual breath.

CHAPTER 25

Alice and Jude have headed out to the kitchen to investigate the coffee situation, and I'm back in Edi's room. Jonah is lying beside her, leafing through a photo album he's brought, pointing out various details of their instamatic 1970s childhood. I lean in to look at a family trip to Greece: here's Edi perched atop a speckled donkey, wearing dusty Mary Janes and white ankle socks; here the kids are in matching white shorts, posing like columns at the Parthenon; here's their dad and his sideburns, biting into an octopus tentacle. "Was that a good trip?" I ask, and Jonah shrugs, says, "Eh."

Edi shifts uncomfortably, rattles the ice in her glass. She clears her throat and doesn't speak. "You need something, sweets?" I say, and she grins at me, rattles the ice in her glass. I sit at the edge of her bed and refill the glass with an open can from the wheelie table. She clears her throat, says, "Um?"

"What's up, pussycat?" I say.

She clears her throat again. "You two are . . ." She points to Jonah and me, stops speaking.

If she says *boning*, I will die before she does. Jonah's eyes have widened into saucers of panic.

Edi clears her throat, rattles the ice. ". . . bartenders?" Jonah catches my eye. "It seems like it, right?" he says. "Another round of Pellegrino for the ladies!"

She nods, then shakes her head. "Not a bar," she says. "The hoozy. The *doily*. Not the doily." She sighs, shakes her head, says, "No." She's quiet again. Jonah pats her shoulder, puts the album down on the bedside table, takes off his glasses to rub his face with his palm, swings his legs over to stand. "I'm going to see what's taking so long with the coffee. You guys want some?" We do! Or at least I do.

After Jonah leaves, Edi looks into my face, studies it. I'm smiling and smiling. She shifts a little, winces, raises her eyebrows and shoulders in alarm. "You're good," I say. "You're perfect." Her shoulders drop, and she smiles.

My kids did this too, when they were little—they looked into my eyes to make sure they were okay. On a turbulent airplane, their two small faces swiveled over to me to ask, wordlessly, "Are we safe?" *We are safe!* I beamed back at them judderingly, because what did it really matter if I was wrong? By the time the plane exploded, the fact that they couldn't trust me anymore would have become quite immediately moot. *You are safe!* I beam at Edi now, and she grins like a jollied baby. "You are doing everything exactly right," I say out loud, and she nods.

Quietly, I sing "Dona, Dona" to her. Every line I remember. *How the winds are laughing, they laugh with all their might! Laugh and laugh the whole day through, and half the summer's night.* When I try to look up more lyrics on my phone, I see that it's actually a song about leading a calf to slaughter. Nice.

Edi's looking at me. She clears her throat. "Ash," she says.

"Edi." Immediately I need to wipe tears from my face with the heel of my hand.

Her eyes focus, fill with something like *herself*. She smiles. "You're such a good friend," she says.

"Oh my god!" I say. I'm crying and smiling so hard my face is breaking apart, my heart is. "You are too. The best."

"The best," she says. I'm holding her hands in my hands. "Stay gold, Ponyboy," she says.

That book—*The Outsiders*—we knew the whole thing practically by heart. When Edi arrived to the first day of her first-year Columbia English class, the professor had written the entirety of "Nothing Gold Can Stay" on the blackboard, asked if anyone knew who the poet was. Edi had raised her hand shyly, smugly, said, "S. E. Hinton." "I think I gave college my best shot," Edi told me that night from the pay phone in her dorm. "And now I'll be packing it up. But seriously, Robert Frost? Ugh. Bite me. Everybody laughed." *Bastards!* From the pay phone in my own dorm, I reminded her that she owned that city—that she was the kind of person who'd grown up reading *Eichmann in Jerusalem* on the 1 train, for god's sake! These snobs had nothing on her. She could outsnob all of them! She was a precious fucking gem, which they would find out soon enough. "Okay, okay," she'd said. "Easy, slugger." But I could hear her pretty smile through the distance.

Nature's first green is gold.

"Edi," I say now. But whatever this is—this window of clarity—it's ending already. Confusion is drawing its bleak curtains. Edi shakes her head, rattles her ice, puts the glass down, and, awkwardly, like her hand is a borrowed hand, pulls a tissue from the box. She passes it to me.

"Thanks, sweetie," I say, wiping my eyes and nose, and she grins at me, lifts her glass, rattles the ice.

The coffee is here now, and Jude and Alice pass a cup to me and set one down on Edi's tray table. Edi grins at them. "Scooch a little," Jude says, and I stand so he can lie down by his wife.

"Oh, shit," he says.

Edi's bag has filled up and disconnected itself from the tube, which is now pouring her stomach contents onto the bed. "Fuck." I shove a plastic bowl under the tube, grab a fresh bag from the shelf, tear open the package, and, once the initial rush has slowed down, attach it to the port. Edi's old bag is on the floor in a spreading pool of pink liquid. Meanwhile, Edi is calmly drinking her soda, rattling her glass, looking at us with huge eyes. I remember to smile at her—the same way I used to try to remember, when the girls were small and covered in barf, that they were miserable, sick kids, not just a daunting disinfection and laundering project. I grab sheets from the linen closet down the hall, grab a blanket from the warmer, ask after a mop, although Violet promises just to send someone in. Jude has tossed a towel over the puddle and is trying to get Edi upright so that we can put fresh sheets on the bed. Miraculously, her nightie is still dry—but we still need to slide the bottom sheet out from under her somehow, which we can't figure out.

"Just put a lap pad over it," a nursing assistant advises. She's come in with the mop. "We'll deal with it later. For now, that's fine. Put the lap pad down, and then a towel over that."

By the time we get Edi comfortable, Jude looks exhausted. "Lie down for a while," I tell him, and he does. Edi shifts a little to face him, and both of them close their eyes. Jonah, Alice, and I decide we'll go and get a little air, grab our coats, and creep out with our cold mugs of coffee.

We walk down the street, toward the park, talking on and off. We're all wondering what happens next. None of us has been with someone when they died: Jonah and Edi's mom died—suddenly, of an aneurysm—while they were both away at college; Alice and I both visited grandmothers in the hospital, but weren't with them during the very last stages.

"I keep thinking of that John Donne poem 'Death Be Not Proud,'" Jonah says. "But I feel more like, 'Death be not so messy and exhausting.'" I feel the same way. I'd pictured something more linear. More constantly, soaringly momentous. Not these dribs and drabs of decline and lucidity. Not so much . . . moisture. I think I imagined a kind of Hallmark card showing two dry hands, clasped dryly. Serenely. But then again, I had the wrong image in my head when I was pregnant too—some idea about newborns that involved a gentle breeze blowing through sunlit curtains, everything white and cottony and powder-scented. Not me nursing an angry, soiled baby on the toilet while I tried to take a dump without also ripping open my many infected stitches. Not the stinking hormonal effluvium from everybody's every pore and orifice. Love, yes, and plenty of it—but *so many fluids.*

While we were inside, though, the earth has turned. Sunshine is pouring from the edge of the sky, and the snow that's left is fizzily disappearing. There's the mineral smell of thaw, the sound of snow-melt tinkling through everybody's gutter. All the trees are heavy with singing birds. The air on my skin feels warm and cool at the same time. Spring is coiled up, ready to . . . Oh my god! Is that why they call it *spring?* "Stop!" I say. "Feel that? We are exactly between two seasons."

"We're definitely between something and something else," Jonah says. "What time is it even?" He looks at his watch. Mystifyingly, it is after five. I remember emerging from the hospital with newborn Jules, and people were just driving their cars and walking around, shopping or leaving work or carrying a bunch of tulips, even though my entire life had been unzipped, emptied, and turned inside out. "Have all these people just been out here this whole time?" I said to

Honey then. "While I was"—I pointed to the hospital—"in *there*, doing *that*?" I pointed to Jules in her car seat. "Making *this*?" "I think pretty much, yeah," Honey answered me, smiling. "I'm guessing time did not stop for anyone but us."

Still, the late hour is baffling even to me.

"I think what we're between," Alice says, "is the Twilight Zone and some other fuckery."

And this is more accurate than we can even understand just yet.

CHAPTER 26

Once we're back at Shapely, Jonah and Alice head inside to check on Edi and forage for snacks. "I'll be in in a sec," I say. "I'm just going to text the girls." But I don't. I sit on the carved wooden bench in the courtyard and tip my face up to the last of the light.

Jude emerges from the back door, shakes his head, says, "Wowza," and sits down heavily next to me. He digs into his pocket for cigarettes, offers me one. "Thank god," I say. I don't smoke, not really, but if it were not an obscenely dangerous pastime I would. I would smoke *a lot*. Jude lights me, and I take a first delicious drag before putting my head between my knees faintingly. "You are still such a ridiculous lightweight," Jude says. He shakes his head. "The one-hit wonder."

The back door opens, and a man and woman come out in overcoats. She bursts into tears, and he stops to turn and wrap her in his arms, but then sees us and apologizes. "Please," I say. "We're the same. This is what it's like." *Every person is a person*, I think redundantly, because my brain is on the *fried* setting. "Take care of yourselves!" we all say as they head for their car. "Good luck!" Oh my god. We're like that stupid balloon.

"You and Honey should get back together," Jude says, as if we've already been talking about this.

I was unable to seduce him, actually, I don't say. Nor do I tell him about Honey singing to me, "Regrets, I've had a few . . ." until I sang back at him, "but then again, too few to mention," and punched him in the arm. What I say instead is, "Honey has a girlfriend," and Jude laughs.

"Ash, whatever. You're sleeping with, like, a hundred people. I just mean in the big picture, I'm rooting for you guys."

"I am not *sleeping with a hundred people*!" I say. "And anyways, who told you I was sleeping with anybody—if I *were* sleeping with anybody, that is?"

Jude smiles at me. "Ash. We've known each other a long time. You're not as mysterious as you might imagine. But also? Edi told me about you and Jonah."

"Oh!" I say. "Wow. *What the actual?*

"She doesn't know if you know that she knows," he says. "But I think she figures, in the scheme of things, it's not that big a deal. She didn't want to freak you out by mentioning it now."

"Okay," I say. "Thank you for telling me, I guess. Do you think I should try to talk to her about it, you know, before"—before *what?*— "too much time passes?"

Jude looks at me, smiles again. "Nah. I don't think it's unfinished business for her. You don't need to worry about it. And she's got"—he hesitates—"a lot on her plate."

Jude lights me another cigarette, even though I'm about to barf from the first one, and we sit quietly, inhaling and exhaling into the deepening blue. I can't tell what kind of silence this is. *When do you think Edi will die?* is a question hanging between us, but it feels faithless to ask it.

"When do you think she's going to die?" Jude says.

I shake my head. "Tonight? A year from now?"

Jude nods. "Right? But if she were a dog, you'd watch her eating that crème brûlée Jonah brought and you'd think, *She's still getting pleasure out of life.*"

"So we shouldn't *euthanize* her is what you're saying?"

Jude laughs. "Yeah, something like that."

"Mom?"

Fuck. It's Jules and Belle. I drop my cigarette behind the bench onto the ground, pray to the slush gods to extinguish it immediately. Jude is grinding his out under his heel.

"Hey, guys!"

"Are you *smoking?*"

Belle looks the way she did when she was little and wandered downstairs in the night and found Honey and me snacking from a gigantic jar of jelly beans we kept hidden in the broom closet. Worse, we weren't just eating them, we were also sorting and trading them by color. Belle was four or five at the time, and she said, furious, "Jules and me go to sleep and then you just eat all the candy and *play with it?*"

I shake my head now, grimace. "I *am* smoking? But I, like, don't *smoke.*"

Belle has her Doc Martens planted in the mud, hands on her hips. In the movie, she would play the scary drill sergeant with a heart of gold. "Mom, I think you *do* smoke if what you're doing is *smoking.*"

"Hey, hey," Jules says, all pink cheeks and heaps of glazy dark curls. "I wonder if we want to put a bookmark here—come back to this conversation a little later. Belle, I'm with you, but look at Mama."

Belle looks at me, and her expression softens. "Oh my god, of course," she says. "I'm sorry. It's fine. We can talk about it another time. How's Edi?"

"Wait," I say. "What? *Look at Mama?*"

Jules leans down to wrap her arms around me, says *pew* about my smoky hair smell, says, "Just that you guys are kind of, you know, *in it*. But how's Edi? Hi, Jude!"

"Hey, Jules, Belle," Jude says. "Edi's in and out. Declining steadily in some ways, right, Ash?" I nod. "And then, I don't know. Less steadily in others. Do you want to say hi?" They do.

In our absence, Shapely has grown stale and sad. It smells like diapers and old cooking oil and something else sour and funky—this might actually be *me*—and none of the lamps have been switched on in the dim living room. Many of the doors are closed, and I hear weeping behind one of them. Back in Edi's room, though, the expensively fragrant candle is aglow, and Cedar has arrived. He's sitting on Edi's bed with his guitar, singing Joni Mitchell. "Hottie alert," Belle says to Jules under her breath, and Jules swats her with her hat but whispers, "Seriously." Jonah and Alice, perched on the deep windowsill, look like zombie extras in a film about zombies.

"We are stardust," Cedar is singing. "We are golden." All of us—we really are! Just a skyful of fourteen-billion-year-old stars that collapsed and supernova-ed their way into our cells via comets and Shakespeare and Chief Tecumseh and whoever all else ever lived and died and decomposed and became human again. And then one day Edi—and the rest of us too, of course—will become something else, someone else. Worms and soil, then a plant, a seed head, maybe, a loaf of bread, a piece of toast, the very stuff of somebody's bones and flesh. And long after, when the earth bursts apart, maybe we become dark matter? Okay, I don't actually know what dark matter is. Belle the mind reader catches my eye, shakes her head, and mouths *crazy*.

Now Cedar is singing the James Taylor lullaby we used to sing the girls. "You can close your eyes, it's all right." Edi, meanwhile, is busy being not conscious. If she's having thoughts and feelings, we have no access to them. Her mouth is open, and, after the song ends, I can hear her breathing. "Geez," Alice says. "She sounds so . . . *rattly*." When nobody responds, she says, "Shit. That's a thing, isn't it. Fuck. I'm sorry." It is, indeed, a thing. Jude wraps a consoling arm around her.

The room feels too crowded, which is probably why Jules says, "Belle, we should head home and feed the cats."

"Good idea," I say. "Thank you. They're probably starving. Are you parked in the front?"

"We walked, actually," Belle says, "which seemed like a good idea at the time."

"Take my car, if you want. There are plenty of cars here."

"Or I could give you guys a ride," Cedar says. "I'm actually heading out too."

"Oh, that would be great!" Jules says, sparkling a little. "Okay, yeah."

Cedar squats down by Edi's bed, takes her hand. "See ya, Edi," he says. He looks up at us shyly, then continues in a low voice, "It has been an honor to play for you." He stands again, moves to the side, and Belle and Jules crowd around the head of Edi's bed. We've always referred to Edi as the girls' *pretend auntie*. The best presents they've ever gotten have come from her: Brooklyn baseball caps and molecular gastronomy kits and coupons to take them out for fancy cupcakes when we came to New York, which she would then always remember to actually do. She has been a steady, loving presence for their entire lives. Now they kiss her slack face, tell her they love her. "I know she loves you guys so much," Jude says. He's crying a little bit, and the girls are too. So am I, it turns out. But when did we all agree that everyone needs to be saying good-bye to her? She'll probably outlive us all!

And yet. I feel it too. Something is humming in Edi, floating off her. You can sense it in the room. Something is changing.

CHAPTER 27

Only that's not the way it goes. Instead, Edi's eyes snap open. She sits up, the pink returning to her cheeks. "Where have I been?" she asks. "What day is it?" The astonished nurses page Dr. Soprano, who arrives and examines her, shakes his head in wonder. "It's the darndest thing!" He says. "There's essentially no evidence of disease!" We laugh and hug each other. Wonder of wonders! Maybe it wasn't even cancer to begin with! It's all been a terrible mistake. Honey grabs me and dips me, kisses me on the lips. We help Edi pack up her stuff, lace up her boots, and she swings out of Shapely, whistling.

If cancer had seen as many romantic comedies as I have, it would understand that what's next on the schedule is *delightful plot twist*. But cancer has mostly just watched gritty documentaries about war and famine. Also melodramas. Cancer has seen *Beaches* and *Terms of Endearment*, and it has no imagination for joy. There will be no turn of events.

Honey is actually here now—although there hasn't been a passionate reconciliation. He's just sitting around, like the rest of us, listening to Edi's gurgly breathing and making occasional small talk. And Dr. Soprano has, in fact, arrived too—but only to sit briefly at the edge of Edi's bed. He cups her chin to look at her face, but he doesn't even examine her. "She's almost certainly passing now," he says. "Passing over. You're all here with her. She has everything she needs." He hugs each of us—he really is such a mensch—and we thank him, tearfully offer him one of Edi's remaining edibles, which he graciously, professionally declines. "I couldn't possibly," he says, and I stop myself from laughing out loud.

"Should we eat something?" Jonah wonders after Dr. Soprano leaves. "It feels stupid to be hungry, but I am, a little." I go to the kitchen, put a block of cheddar and some crackers on a plate, bring it back to the room. Farrah click-clacks back in after me, but then she sniffs around Edi's bed and creeps out again, cheeselessly.

"That's unsettling," Jude says. It really is.

"What was the last thing she actually said?" Alice asks. "Does anybody know?" And Jude says, "Dash. Just that. *Dash.*"

How do I tell this part? We pass each other crackers with cheese. We listen to Edi breathe. I rub her lips with a sponge swab for no particular reason, wipe her face with a warm washcloth. Jonah and Jude are each holding one of her hands now. Honey is holding one of mine. I hold one of Alice's. And then we are singing. We sing "Hallelujah." The windows are fully dark now, the only light in the room glowing from the candle. We sing "The Long and Winding Road." We take turns telling Edi how much we love her. We tell her we know she has a long journey ahead of her, that she can go whenever she needs to, that we'll take good care of Dash. This is love, distilled to its essence—like a kind of communal ecstasy, but grief. We sing "Let It Be" and, when we finish, we listen into the silence for Edi to inhale.

But she doesn't. She's leaving behind the shell of her human flesh, molting like an invisible butterfly, disappearing. She's going, she's gone. You could almost grab onto her wings and go too.

I put a hand on her chest and feel the stillness where her heart should be beating. And then I put a hand to mine. And here's my own unruly heart, thumping away. On and on, heartlessly.

CHAPTER 28

Much later, Jude rejoins us at the house. We're all still awake, wired and drained, like little overtired kids who spent too long at the fair, if the fair were a place people went to snack on ice cream bars and then die. We're eating and drinking, laughing and crying, breathing in and out—all the things alive people do, I guess. Belle is sitting sleepily against me in her red onesie pajamas. Cedar is here too, perched on an ottoman next to Jules, who catches my eye and winks because a beloved somebody shuffling off their mortal coil is no reason not to invite the hot boy inside, as I well know.

Jude is wrecked. He tells us that a minute after we all left, as he was sitting with Edi, he'd gotten a text from Dash. *Did Mom die?* It was after two in the morning. When he called back, Dash absorbed the news quietly, then explained that Edi had shaken him awake and kissed him, held him in her arms before disappearing again.

"Shit," I say. "That's crazy."

"I know," Jude says.

"She stopped to see Dash on her way out," I say. "I love that."

"Me too," Jude says. "So much."

"Fuck," I say. "Edi died."

"I know," Jude says again.

It's occurring to me only now that the dying and the loss are actually two different burdens, and each must be borne individually, one after the other. It's like after a grueling delivery, when they hand it to you and you're like, *Oh! The baby!* because your focus had become so narrow and personal during the birth. But now here was the actual end point, which you'd always known but then forgotten in all of the incarnated drama and suffering.

It's been so arduous, Edi's dying. It's like we've all been digging and digging, shoveling out a hole, and we can finally stop. Only now there's this hole here.

Which is no reason not to make French toast! Or so seems to be the thinking of Honey and Belle, who are in the kitchen, frying up platters full of it, custardy and buttery and perfect, plates and forks and maple syrup passed around the living room. Honey has also cut a couple of pink grapefruits into skinny half-moons, and it's just what I didn't know I needed: bracing and delicious. Cedar has his guitar out, and he and Jules are singing quietly together with Jonah, "Hey Jude," and all the other Edi favorites. *Okay, okay*, I think, to nobody in particular. *Consider life affirmed.* It's also possible that I'm drunk.

By the time Alice notices that the sky is lightening, we're stuffed and fading, but we all bundle up and head out to the tippy top of the meadow to watch the sun come up in bands of color: blue first, then purple, pink, orange, pink again. We sing "Here Comes the Sun" and cry. I beg everybody to stay forever, and then—except for Honey, who breaks my broken heart by heading home—we all pile back into the house and go immediately to bed. Bizarrely, nobody especially needs to get up for anything. Belle squeezes in beside me on the couch, says, "Squeeze my arm like a blood pressure cuff," but is asleep before I've even wrapped my hands around her bicep. But I can't seem to close my eyes. It is March second.

CHAPTER 29

Luckily, my mom is narrow as a toothpick, because Jules and Belle and I are all crammed with her into the back seat of the car like hulking girl giants. My dad is up front with Honey, who is driving us from the Upper West Side to Brooklyn, where we will be attending the funeral of my best friend, who has been dead for two days. Despite this impossible fact, my father has many unsolicited opinions to share about Honey's choice of route.

"The West Side Highway?" my dad says. "This is totally screwy. We should be on the FDR."

"As you mentioned," I say.

"I'm looking at the app, Grandpa," Jules says gently, from beneath Belle. "Dad's going the way it suggests. It looks like there's some bananas traffic on the FDR."

"I'm not talking about an app. I'm just saying that the FDR is how you get to Brooklyn."

"Oh my god, Dad," I say. "Please." I have heard my father offer so many opinions about routes over the years that I can, on demand, recall the sound of his voice saying the words *Throgs Neck Bridge*. "I never really thought about a frog's *neck* before," Jules said in the car when she was little, and then, a year or two later, Belle said, "Wait. Frogs have *necks*?"

My dad throws up his hands. "Okay, okay. You don't need to get so exercised," he says. "I'm just saying we're going to be late because of this screwy route."

"Hey, Grandpa," Jules says. "Maybe just sit back and relax? I think my mom is losing it a little bit."

My dad turns in his seat to look at me, and, indeed, I am losing it a little bit. I smile at him, but I can feel that my cheeks are wet with tears. "Oh, honey," he says, and then, "Not you," to Honey, which is an old favorite joke of his. "Are you crossing at Fifty-Ninth?" he adds.

"Abe," my mother says crisply—somehow even the single syllable is enough to daunt everybody, maybe because she's English—and my father says, "Okay, okay. I'm just asking."

I can't see her because of these enormous girls between us, but I whisper, "Thanks, Mom."

I remember once when Honey and I were barely still together, picking up a greeting card from my mother's bedside table. It was pretty on the front—blooming cherry trees in Central Park maybe—and then inside it just said, in my dad's scratchy handwriting, *Happy 51st anniversary, love of my life.* Not, *I know this year's been hard, but . . .* Not proliferating sentences about what commitment means and why. Just that.

My dad asks the girls to remind him about everybody's name—"Edi's kid—it's a girl?"—before apologizing for his Alzheimer's, which he doesn't have. "I keep forgetting what it's called, so I have a mnemonic for it. *Al's hammer.*" "You have a mnemonic device to re-member *Alzheimer's*," Belle says. "Oh my god, Grandpa." He laughs. I try to look at the eulogy without making myself carsick. It's either too long or too short, and there are still parts I'm really not sure about.

"It's okay, Mama," Jules says to me, a little muffled by Belle's down jacket, which is pressed into her face. "It's not, like, material you're being tested on. You'll just do your best, and it will be amazing."

"Thank you, sweetie," I say, with incredible restraint, because this child! She is a national fucking treasure.

Honey drops us all off at the synagogue before parking. "Now we're *early*, for Christ's sake," my Dad says. Jonah and Alice and Jude and Dash are there, clumped on the sidewalk. I am holding my mom's arm to help her up over the curb, but I want to run to them. *My people.*

"My people!" I cry out. I am crying and crying. "Aaaaaugh, this boy," I say, squeezing Dash and lifting him off the ground. He says, "Ash!" and laughs. His hair is combed, and he's wearing a coat and tie and also—soccer shorts? And dirty pink Crocs. Edi's been dead for two days, and it's already all going to shit. Or else, maybe, it is absolute perfection.

The girls hug Dash too, and my mom is hugging everybody, crying a little bit, saying how dreadfully sorry she is. My dad shakes Jude's hand, shakes Jonah's, shakes his head. "Ucch," he says. "I'm sorry. It's terrible. Just terrible." I lean my head against his familiar shoulder. I can feel how embarrassed he is to be so old and alive. My beloved father.

"Edi's dad?" I whisper to Jude, who tells me he's inside with the rabbi.

Other mourners are arriving now, and we cannot monopolize these people, so we head inside to find seats. "Sit up front," Jude yells after me. "Even if somebody tells you different."

Somebody does, but we do. And after a bit, the service starts. A projected photo of Edi appears on a screen, and everyone gets to hear my father loudly whispering into the sudden silence, "I was never a big fan of that particular hairstyle." My mother shushes him. The rabbi, who is a woman and who has a beautiful voice, sings "You Must Believe in Spring," stepping aside in the middle so that Dash can play a blattingly exquisite solo on his trumpet. There is not a dry eye in the house. Jonah does a comedic reading of a single letter that Edi sent him from camp one summer. It's mostly a catalogue of complaints about the latrines and the bugs and the food, including a line we've quoted for decades: "You call *this* an alfredo sauce?"

Jude takes the microphone to describe Edi's most recent work: a film with the working title *The Unfinished Scarf Project*, but which we now all refer to as *The* Unfinished *Unfinished Scarf Project*. He screens a clip for us. In it, an ancient afghan-draped woman on a park bench in Brooklyn is explaining how the idea came to her: that all these people were picking up knitting and crocheting but then putting it down again—quitting projects halfway through. "All over the city!" she says. "So many unfinished scarves! So my granddaughter helped me—whatchamacallit—make a Google about it." She adjusts her glasses and smiles, presumably at Edi behind the camera. "And now we collect the unfinished scarves and we finish them. There's a group of us. And then we auction them off to raise money for our homeless youth." "How much money have you raised?" you hear Edi ask, and the woman ducks her head shyly, says, "Believe it or not, a little more than a million dollars," and then you hear Edi laugh, and it is such a pure, ringing expression of her delight that I burst into tears again. *Edi.*

"Wait. What?" I'm saying to Jude, who has said something to me from the podium, and he smiles, says, "It's you. You're up, Ash." Oh!

As soon as the mic's in my hand, I'm crying. Laughing and crying both, before I utter a single word. Finally, I say, "Well, that went pretty well, actually!" and people laugh. I tell everybody gathered that Edi had excellent taste in friends—I pause here, to make them laugh again, and also to drive Edi crazy, but, hey, if she didn't want my eulogy to be all about me, she could have stuck around to make sure—and also excellent taste in parents and siblings, husbands and children. That she was brilliant and loyal, beautiful, sometimes humble. That she loved to listen and laugh. That she was generous and also exacting. That she expected a lot from all of us, and we tended to rise to the occasion that was her way of being in the world. I quote her beloved Beatles: *And in the end, the love you take is equal to the love you make.* "She made—and took—a lot of it," I say.

And then I turn to Dash, because this is what I'm here to do. I tell him the same thing I told his mom at Shapely: that she joyfully devoted her life to feeding him—figuratively, of course, but mostly literally. I describe how, when he was a toddler, she would arrive at our house for the weekend and immediately begin cutting fruit into tiny unchokable chunks—peaches and plums, nectarines and bananas, everything diced up into these benignly nourishing one-millimeter cubes—and this cutting of the fruit would last pretty much throughout the entire weekend because Dash really, really loved fruit, and Edi really, really didn't want him to choke. "But also," I'm saying to him, "she just really loved doing it. Feeding you. And maybe you carry her with you now not only in your memories, but in the actual cells of your body." I try to steady my breathing. "All that love," I say. "It's in your very blood and bones. It's what you're made out of. So she's still here with you, Dash, with all of us. Even though we are going to miss her so, so much."

When I get back to my seat, Honey reaches behind Belle to squeeze my shoulder, and the girls tearfully wrap their arms around me.

My damp-eyed father leans over Jules with an Altoids tin. "Careful," he whisper-yells as I reach for a mint. "There's a hearing aid battery in there. And a Valium."

A minute later I hear him say to Jules, "I don't know what that is—a Skittles party," and Belle, on my other side, laughs out loud.

"It's a young-people drugs thing," she says, and my father shrugs and leans over Jules to pat me consolingly. "That was great," he says to me—which is actually more than I can take. I'm crying and somehow there's mint up in my nose and all I can say is, "Thanks, Dad."

CHAPTER 30

We don't go to the cemetery because Edi is not getting buried. This is a point of contention. She'd wanted to be cremated—to have her ashes scattered in Central Park, in Prospect Park, at Coney Island—but this is not a traditional Jewish practice, and a compromise has been reached: she will be cremated, and then, at a later date, the urn full of ashes will be buried. "It's kind of neither here nor there," Jude says, between bites of an everything bagel spackled with whitefish salad. We're at their house for the first night of shiva. "Honestly?" he says. "It doesn't really matter a whole ton to me." Even chewing, Jude looks so tired that his face is essentially falling off the front of his head. If there's a patron saint of the exhausted I should pray to her for both of us. "If Dash wants, I'll sneak out a handful of ashes and he can fling them somewhere. I'll sneak you one too," he adds, since I must have a *What about me?* expression on my face like usual.

I look over at Dash, who is conked out in Jules's lap. Belle is next to them on the couch, and on their other side is Cedar because he *had to be in New York anyway*, and wanted to just *pop by and pay his respects to Edi's late husband* (nobody corrects him). "*Somebody's* got to be banging Edi's support staff," Belle whispered to me, since I myself have sworn off this particular style of grief management. "It might as well be Jules."

Now Belle lifts a black ceramic tube from the coffee table, holds it up to one eye, and turns it slowly. "This kaleidoscope suuucks," she says.

Dash opens his eyes, giggles sleepily. "I think that's actually just a vase, Belle," he says, and she nods, says, "That makes sense at least."

"I dreamed about her last night," I say to Jude quietly.

"Oh my god, me too!" Jude says. "You first."

In my dream, I tell him, she called me from Shapely. "You haven't visited me in days!" she said, and I said, "Oh my god! I'm so sorry. I thought you were actually . . . uh . . . *not receiving visitors*." Jude laughs.

"What about you?" I say, and he says, "Same. I was smoking in the yard and she was there, suddenly, standing in the doorway. I hid the cigarette behind my back. *Oh! Hi! I didn't expect to see you!*"

"Can we just dream that she's alive and not disappointed in us?" I ask him, and he says, "Apparently not."

At some point I go upstairs to use Edi and Jude's bathroom. Edi's perfume is in there, and I want to spritz some into the air, onto my hands—to breathe in the smell of her. But when I stop to look at the framed photographs that are back up on the bedroom wall, I hear a muffled sound. Everybody's coats are piled on Edi's bed, but a person is there too, half underneath all the outerwear. It's Edi's dad.

"Myron?" I go to him, and he holds a hand out to me. I take it and sit, stroke his knuckles.

"Ash," he says. "Ash, my heart is breaking." He sounds so much like Edi that my breath catches.

"Oh, Myron," I say. "Oh, I know. I can only imagine. Mine too— but *yours*. Your beautiful daughter. I'm so sorry."

"We shouldn't have even done it," he says vaguely. *Had Edi* is what he might mean.

I sit quietly, imagining his face covered in hearts, glittering with stardust. *Is* it better to have loved and lost? Ask anyone in pain and they'll tell you no. And yet. Here we are, hurling ourselves headlong into love like lemmings off a cliff into a churning sea of grief. We risk every last thing for our heart's expansion, even when that expanded heart threatens to suffocate us and then burst. I need to find my kids. I need to sit here with Myron while grief tries to swallow him whole.

Unbeknownst to anybody, I have applied to nursing school and been accepted. I've talked to the director at Shapely, told her, half joking—but only half—that I'll be back in a couple of years, that she should hold a job for me. What I'm starting to understand, finally, is that the point isn't to help the people who know how best to ask for help. It's to be helpful. I tell Myron that he's connecting the wrong dots. "Not wrong," I clarify. "But you're tracing only a picture of grief, of your own broken heart. But really, all the stars are there, and they're showing you the joy too. You can make the Edi's-smile con-stellation, the one shaped like Dash, like Jonah. Every single thing."

Myron lets me continue to hold his hand while his tears pool on everybody's coats. He nods. And meanwhile I'm connecting the stars that spell *Honey*. Even though he's already tattooed on my heart.

Jonah has come in quietly, sits on the bed by me and his dad. "Let me stay with him awhile," he says to me, which is good. Because I have to find my husband.

I run into him on the stairs. He's coming up to find me. "Honey!" I say.

"Ash." I'm standing one step above him. We're eye to eye. "Ash, be with me," he says. "Please." All the cells in my body turn toward him, like a school of fish in sunlight. Like iron filings rearranging themselves for a beloved magnet.

"What about Gemma?" I say.

"Gemma dumped me," he says cheerfully, and I say cheerfully back, "Oh, that's too bad! Why?"

"Why do you think?"

"Because the entirety of your New Year's resolution was to not floss with a too-short piece of floss?" I say, and he shakes his head. "Because you're in love with me." I'm dizzy as I say it.

"Because I'm in love with you," he says. He sits, pulls me awkwardly into his lap, wraps his arms around me, and kisses my neck, my jaw.

"Reunited is not going to feel so good when we fall down the stairs and break our necks," I say. "Plus, Edi will kill me if I die at her shiva."

"Oh my god, you guys." It's Belle, of course, looking up at us from the bottom of the staircase. "Jesus, Mom. You're banging *Dad* now?"

"Isabelle," I say. "I am not *banging* your father."

"Ewwww," she says. "Don't even say it." But she's grinning like a cartoon pirate.

"Oh my!" It's my mother now, standing beside Belle. "I was coming to check on you," she says. "But, well. Here you are!" I stand, and Honey stands after me. "Your father and I are going to say our good-byes and steal away."

"Let me drive you," Honey says.

"Oh, thank you, Honey love," my mother says. "We'll just take the subway. I think Abe wants to stop at that bakery anyway. The place with the Portuguese rolls. You know he doesn't mind a bit of a journey if there's food involved."

I walk down the stairs to lean against her. "I'm sorry," I say vaguely. I'm not entirely sure what for. Being a weirdo, being a skank. Being the happy-saddest person who ever lived. "Don't be, darling," she says. "Life is messy. I certainly don't expect tidiness from yours or anybody else's." She kisses the side of my head. Then she wraps her arms around me because I'm crying. Honey's got an arm draped over Belle's shoulder, but he uses his other hand to tuck my hair behind my ear. Everything is unspooling inside me now. If I were a ball of yarn, I'd be just a stringy tangle on the floor. If I were a reservoir, I'd be overflowing my banks. Who I really need to talk to about all of this, of course, is Edi.

"She's going to miss *everything* now," I sob.

"And you're going to miss her," my mother says. "Such lucky girls, both of you."

This is true and not at all true. Plus, I'm so, so tired. But also? Maybe I'm waking up.

CHAPTER 31

Belle has threatened to make me a T-shirt that says, MY BEST FRIEND
DIED AND ALL I GOT WERE THESE STUPID UGG BOOTS. But I got more
than that. So much more.

Like, for example, all of her dresses and yoga pants, one of her
Columbia hoodies, some flannel pajama bottoms, a bunch of T-shirts
that were actually mine, including, yes, my SAVE THE WHALES T-shirt,
a tube of her scented hand lotion, and most of her unvaluable jewelry,
including the many groovy anklets I seem to have made her over the
years from bells and seashells and my own nag champa–scented optimism.

"Really, anything," Jude had said to me and Alice. The three of us
were inside the vast, Edi-smelling closet. "I already put a few things
aside for Dash. Help yourselves to whatever you want." He'd left
us to it.

Alice had looked around a bit and then whispered, "Doesn't it feel
kind of weird?"

"It doesn't?" I said. "But I totally get that. I mean, it probably
should? But no." The girls had already headed back up to Massachusetts with Honey—Jules had to get back to school—and I was going

to get a ride the next day from Cedar. Alice wandered off to investigate the leftover-smoked-fish situation. And then I was alone in my underpants in Edi's closet, putting on her clothes. Costuming myself as the kind of person who could live on the planet without her.

Here was her wedding dress—with all of its hastily sewn-on buttons—in a zippered bag. And here was the slinky, satiny champagne-colored dress she wore to mine. I remember talking to the florist about colors that would look good with both of our dresses. My mom, an avid gardener, had suggested everlasting as a nice filler for the bouquet, and the florist said, "Well, I've got *pearly* everlasting, *early* everlasting, and *clammy* everlasting. Which do you want?" I'd said something about *clammy everlasting* not feeling like a great omen for a marriage, and he hadn't laughed. "I guess pearly?"

There's a picture of Edi and me from my wedding day, shoving cake in each other's faces while Honey, baby-faced and grinning, stood nearby. He'd catered our reception: tied up fifteen loins of pork with rosemary and white kitchen string; picked, steamed, and buttered a dozen pounds of green beans; and candied countless violets and rose petals to decorate the layers of chocolate cake he'd baked and frosted. He actually had to excuse himself from the very beginning of the ceremony—really, the music had barely started, and everybody laughed when he held one finger up sheepishly and then sprinted across the lawn in his suit—because the onions had caught fire in the makeshift pizza oven, and his assistant was waving to him from the blaze. We were so young, all of us. Edi in her whole, well body with only tiny little scars still, like the one beneath her chin from falling off a balance beam in fifth grade. Scars that represented only healed injuries.

By the time I emerged from the closet, I had filled an enormous bag with Edi's things. "I'm sorry I'm so shameless," I said to Jude, and he said, "Not at all. I'm glad. You'll wear it in good health," and hugged me.

Now, home again, I'm sitting at the kitchen table with a glass of delicious red wine—I've opened one of the bottles we never drank with Edi—writing thank-you notes to everyone at Shapely. Belle is making her famous bean feast, which is really just a pot of perfect pintos that she serves with lots of toppings: feta and fruity olive oil, cilantro and diced avocado, pickled radishes and pickled jalapeños. It's as good a meal as you could possibly eat.

"Is *shout-out* one word?" I ask her, and she yells, "Scrotum!"

"What?" she says when I look at her blankly. "You said, 'Shout out one word.'"

Everything (except Belle) is different from how it was. It's like I walked back into my own home backwards, and have stayed backwards ever since. Or like somebody rearranged all the furniture. Actually, somebody *did* rearrange all the furniture—Honey and Belle have moved the couches around so that there's more space to play games on the carpet in front of the woodstove—but it's not just that, of course. It's the deep well of nothing where Edi should be, like if you poked a painful tooth with your tongue, only the tooth was gone, and then you got sucked, tongue-first, into a black hole. I stash thoughts and experiences in my mental Edi file to talk to her about later, and then realize that they'll stay there forever. This is more confusing to me than it should be.

Honey's not all the way back in the house yet, though he will be soon. He's going to rent his little apartment above the shop to Cedar, and then he'll finish moving home. For now, though, it's like falling in love again. Or maybe it just *is* falling in love again. I space out, during the day, thinking about our nights together. I kiss him goodbye at the door, kiss him hello, breathe him in, cry beneath him, sleep deeply beside him, wake up infatuated. The girls are overjoyed and also a little mad again that we split up in the first place. That might actually describe how Honey feels too, to be honest.

"You were more than a physician to us," I write in my card to Dr. Soprano, then tear it up. Everything feels like a skit from *The Benny Hill Show*. The same thing happens when I use the expression *above and beyond* to thank Jen and the rest of the volunteers. Here's my etiquette advice about how to write a good thank-you note: Don't have slept with everybody.

Belle eyes the growing pile of torn-up note cards, points to the Disney villain stamps on all my envelopes: Cruella de Vil, Jafar, Maleficent. Laughs at me. "Let's get some air," she says. "Come outside with me. Dad won't be home for another hour, and the beans are on low."

It's been so mild. The light rain that's falling stirs up a particular rain-on-the-sidewalk smell I associate with summer. "There's a word for that," Belle says when I mention it. "*Petrichor*. Which would be a great band name, actually." It really would. The dogwood buds are swelling; the meadow is greening up; the season is changing or has already changed.

My jacket pockets are full of shopping lists. I can feel them with my fingertips. They're documents of Edi's discomfort and pleasure: watermelon, Italian ice, good chocolate with sea salt, lip balm, maxi pads, champagne, egg salad. Evidence of her desires, her existence. I can't bring myself to recycle them, but can't think where to put them. So for now they're just here, in my pockets. Maybe I'll put this jacket back on in the fall, and they'll still be there. That's okay, though, right?

Belle has jogged up ahead to investigate something growing on a stump at the side of the meadow. "Chicken mushrooms!" she yells excitedly. They're bright orange and edible, and she breaks off a huge shelf of them, then turns to run back to me. I open my arms instinctively, and she runs into them like the toddler she was so long ago. My whole life with the girls is telescoped into this moment—running away, running back. *Fly, be free!* I want to say. I want to say, *Stay with me forever!* Come to think of it, these are the two things I want to say to everyone I love most.

"That's a great haul," I say, and she says, "I know!" She tucks the fungus under one arm and uses her free hand to take mine. She'll sliver up these mushrooms and fry them in butter, serve them alongside the beans. Her father will join us for this perfect meal, then he will join me in our bed, where we will whisper and laugh. Where we will be broken and also whole. Where we will gently sing Tevye and Golde's song "Do You Love Me?" back and forth while I cry over everything lost and, miraculously, not lost. Where I will, finally, rest.

I dreamed last night that Edi was visiting everybody in their dreams: Jude, Dash, Jonah, Alice. *Did she come to you? Yes! Me too!* Everybody but me. In the dream I talked to Laura from Shapely about it. "Maybe you're not trying hard enough," she said, and I said, "I don't know how to try harder." Laura shrugged. "Hey, she's doing her best," somebody said from behind her. *Edi!* She was palely opalescent, smiling. "You're good, Ash, you're perfect," she said, before kissing my cheek and leaving me again. "You are doing everything right." And it wouldn't be true forever, but, in that moment at least, it was. It was true enough.

ACKNOWLEDGMENTS

My expansively lovely US editor, Sara Nelson, was all in from the beginning and stayed that way, and working with her has been like a wonderful dream (not that I have actual wonderful dreams ever, but I'm imagining). My patient, faithful agent, Jennifer Gates, is a brilliant reader, advocate, and confidante, and she also thought of the title (of course). Everyone at Aevitas has my back, but Erin Files, Allison Warren, and Shenel Ekici-Moling have it very especially, as does Rachel Clements at Abner Stein in the UK. I am grateful to everyone over at Harper, including Maya Baran, Katie O'Callaghan, Sacha Chadwich, Mary Gaule, Alicia Gencarelli, and Edie Astley. In the UK, I've been blessed with this genius Doubleday team, which includes the loveliest Kirsty Dunseath (whose original email I treasure), Alison Barrow, Louis Patel, and Beci Kelly, who designed such a perfectly, deliciously damaged cover. Thank you also, dear librarians and booksellers, for getting books into people's hands.

The actual heroes, my beloved people: David and Simone Van Taylor; Jesse and Nate Pomeroy; Jeremy and Jordana Pomeroy; Sarah and the late, great Lee Pomeroy. Amanda Gronich and Eve-Laure Ortega. Amy Rosenthal. The worst possible thing; the best possible humans.

Hospice is an amazing place. My favorite, ha ha ha, but actually! The incredible staff and residents of Menorah, where Ali died, and the Fisher Home, where I cook Monday dinners, have inspired me to no end with their courage, compassion, terrible humor, and enormous, messy humanity. Palliative care doctors and the fearlessly loving nurses and CNAs keep us alive and then help us die—everything, and with all the grace in the world.

In real life, the "local friends" were (and are) so much more than a passing mention. I'm sorry I laugh-cried so much snot into your hair: Emily Bloch, Nicole Blum, Ava Blum-Carr, Lee Bowie, Pengyew Chin, Dan Costello, Sarah Dolven, Khalid Elkalai, Chris Felton, Judy Frank, Viveca Greene, Daniel Hall, Jagu Jagannathan, Jill Kaufman, Becky Michaels, Meredith Michaels, Colleen Osten, Chris Perry, Lydia Peterson, Brittany Shahmehri, and Kathleen Traphagen. Thank you for feeding and loving and listening to and singing with me during the long season of my breaking heart.

Over the course of an endless, snowy pandemic winter of writing, Maddie DelVicario and Corn Walker offered me absolute sustenance out of doors, like a kind of Shackleton-themed potato-soup party. The Amherst Tire Running Club always gave me something to look forward to. Lydia Elison kept me sane (OR TRIED TO), and Jennifer Rosner cheered me on.

Seemingly permanent faith in me provided, as always, by the motley OG tribe: Andrew Coburn, Kelly Close, Judy Haas, Ann Hallock, Sam Marion, Rebecca Morgan, Anna Paganelli, and Emily Todd. Also, my faithful, newly menopausal, spitfire readers from the Bringing Up Ben and Birdy days. You guys! Honestly.

Folks who have kept me happily employed so I could write for cash as well as love include Sally Sampson, everyone at *Real Simple* (including Liz Vaccariello, Anna Maltby, Kristin van Ogtrop, Rory Evans, Noel Howey, and Elizabeth Passarella), the diaTribe Foundation, and the Amherst College Creative Writing Center—among many other editors and clients who have made my life po$$ible. Thank you Roberta Zeff, Lindsey Mead, Jennifer Niesslein, Amanda Fields, and Rachel Moritz for commissioning the various (weird) essays that made me think I could write (weirdly) about this.

Friends (and a daughter) who generously helped me through my various writing-specific problems include KJ Dell'Antonia, Jess Lahey, the #AmWriting Facebook group (who taught me you're never too old for a sticker chart), Amity Gaige, Katherine Center, Cammie McGovern, Birdy Newman, Sabrina Callahan, and the fierce, funny, and gracious Laura Tisdel. *All My Puny Sorrows* is the funniest-saddest book of the funny-sad books, and I'm lucky that my idol Miriam Toews wrote it.

I am beyond grateful for my faithfully doting all-weather parents, Ted and Jennifer Newman, who taught me to be loving and resilient by being that way themselves. For my world-changing brother and sister-in-law, Robert Newman and Alba Vilajeliu, and beautiful, hilarious nephews, Sam, Lucas, and Andreu. And for my absolute champion father-in-law, Larry Millner.

Snapper Cat, Jellyfish, and the (badly missed) Craney Crow comforted all of us with their ceaseless, smelly purring.

And, above all: Michael, Ben, and Birdy. Thank you for being sad with me when I'm sad, for being happy with me when I'm happy, and for laughing at me when I'm just a total monster of weirdness. You are the most fun, loving, and generous people, my actual everything, and I stole all the best lines from you, as you know.

Ali Pomeroy, wherever you are. Come back to me.

ABOUT THE AUTHOR

CATHERINE NEWMAN is the author of the memoirs *Catastrophic Happiness* and *Waiting for Birdy*, and the bestselling children's book *How to Be a Person*. She writes the etiquette column for *Real Simple* magazine, and is a regular contributor to the *New York Times*, *O, The Oprah Magazine*, *Parents* magazine, and many other publications. She lives in Amherst, Massachusetts, with her family.

The new novel from Catherine Newman, publishing in June 2024.

**One week in Cape Cod.
The perfect family holiday.
What could possibly go wrong?**

**Sandwiched between her adolescent
children and ageing parents,
Rocky is about to find out.**

To be published in June 2024.

Read on

for

an extract . . .

When you think of Cape Cod, you might picture lapis skies or skies tiered in glorious bands of gray. You might picture wild stretches of beach backed by rugged dunes or quaintly shingled houses with clouds of blue hydrangea blossoming all over the place. You might picture the deep, steel blue of the sea as the setting sun puddles into it in melting-popsicle colors. Which is funny, because most of the time you're actually at the surf shop or the weird little supermarket that smells like raw meat, or in line at the clam shack, the good bakery, the porta-potty, the mini-golf place. You're buying twenty-dollar sunscreen at the gas station. You're waiting for your child to pick out six pieces of saltwater taffy with the beach in a querying thought bubble above your head while your beard turns white and grows down to the floor, pages flying off the calendar. You're waiting at the walk-in clinic because the kids have sudden fevers and, it turns out, strep throat; you're waiting at the old-fashioned pharmacy for the ancient pharmacist to mix up—or maybe *invent*—the antibiotics that will make everyone need to lean out from their narrow beds with the anchor-printed coverlets and barf feverishly into the speckled enamel lobster pot you've placed on the floor between them. But also, yes, beaches and ponds and epic skies. All of it.

"I think I'm just getting these again." Jamie is holding out a pair of black board shorts in the hand his girlfriend, Maya, isn't holding.

"Great," I say. "I'm really glad you packed your own swimsuit," I say to Maya. "Feel free to get something if you want, though!"

"I'm good," she says, "but thank you."

Maya, like Jamie and Willa and young people every-where, is a perfect human specimen. Her hair cascades—It actually *cascades!*—over her shoulders in shiny black curls in a way that makes me reach back to feel my own damp ponytail, as narrow as your grandma's crochet hook. Her skin glows and gleams. She's got a pair of tiny silver hoops in one perfect nostril and a pair of enormous silver hoops in her two perfect ears. She's wearing just the merest suggestion of cut-offs and also a garment that is, I think, a bra—but which I'm told is a *bralette*, which means it is a shirt. I am here for all of it—the young people and their bodies. I wish I'd dressed like that when I was their age instead of in the burlap sack dresses we favored for their astonishing shapelessness. "What's in there?" people surely wondered. *A youthful human torso and legs? A truckload of Idaho potatoes?* There was no telling.

"I'm glad you're here," I say, smiling at Maya, and she says, "Me too."

"I'm just going to get these same ones I got last year." Nick is holding out a pair of black board shorts that is either similar or identical to Jamie's. Willa's getting a gray sports bra and the same shorts as her father and older brother.

"Okay, okay," I say. "Shit. You guys are fast. I've got to try some stuff on. I don't even know what size I am this year." I look down as if the top view of my boobs is going to resolve into a numeral. "Help me. I need something with, I don't know, some kind of padding? Some kind of *compression* something or other."

"Just get one that's comfortable, Mama," Willa says. "Or you're going to be picking it out of your ass crack and mad at Dad the whole time about forgetting the swimsuits." This is probably true. I run my hands over the rack of one-pieces, and I am suddenly remembering buying a suit here twenty years ago, when Jamie was three and I was very pregnant with Willa. My boobs were enormous again. When I'd gone to put on the tankini I'd worn through multiple summers of pregnancy and nursing, the taxed elastic had made that sad ripping sound, the one that means it won't be snapping back again after. Come to think of it, I'm surprised my actual body doesn't make that sound every time I bend over.

"What?" Willa says. She's looking at my face. "What's going on with you, besides being concussed or whatever you are?"

"How are you an adult?" is one question I don't ask. "Are all those little girls nested inside you like Matryoshka dolls?" is another. All those summers of the kids with their sticky hands and sticky faces and excitedness! "Just sentimental," I say instead, and kiss her perfect, rosy empath cheek. I try on two different sizes of the same navy-blue one piece. ("Keep your underpants on!" Willa yells helpfully into the fitting room because when my generation was her age, we probably went nudely into the changing cabinet to infect all the woolen swimming costumes with syphilis.) The suit that doesn't squinch my groin is gappy at the chest. I jog in place and it's not good. One big wave and my boobs will definitely be celebrating their dangly freedom. The one that's a snugger fit, though, feels like it's going to pinch my legs all the way off. It also bisects my butt in a way that makes it look like I have two distinct sets of ass cheeks. The more the merrier! But actually, less merry.

You are on unceded Wampanoag territory someone has written on the door in Sharpie. My aging body is not going to change the course of history one way or another. I pick the roomier suit.

"That was a fun two hundred dollars to spend!" I say in the car, and everyone grumbles at me to let it go.

"Check your privilege," Willa says, and I can't tell if she's teasing or not—but she's right.

"That's fair," I say. "Is it *check* like check it at the door? Or *check* like take a good, hard look?"

"I don't know," Willa says. "Just pick one and do it."

"Beach?" Nick says. "Dinner? What's everyone feeling like?" What everyone is feeling like is quick beach and then clam shack. Nick signals to turn toward the bay.

"Wait," I say, craning around to talk to Jamie. "Did you tell Daddy about your work—the nice thing your supervisor said?"

"Ew, Mom," Willa says.

"What?"

"Don't call him *Daddy*."

"Oh right," I say. "I forgot that we're not supposed to say *daddy*. Even in the car, when it's just us. We might think we're sex trafficking each other!"

"Do you guys even know what daddy means?"

"Yes, Willa. We know what *daddy* means." Do we, though? I'm not actually sure. I mean, I'm the same person who thought the Fleetwood Mac song "Oh, Daddy" was about Stevie Nicks' father, to whom she seemed to be unusually devoted. Nick looks at me quickly, and grimaces, shrugs.

"Okay, then, tell your peepaw," I say to Jamie, who laughs and says, "I think I'll just tell him later."

When we get down to the water's edge, the sun is disappearing behind pink-and-blue cotton-candy clouds. The sand is damp and cool, freckled with dark stones and white bits of shell. There are only a handful of other people, everyone turned toward the horizon. We hold up towels so that Nick and Willa can take turns changing into their new suits, both of them tearing off tags in a way that makes me cringe. "Don't rip the fabric!" I don't say, because duh. The rest of us watch from the shore as they run screaming together through the froth. I see Willa wrap her arms around his neck so that Nick can bounce her in the waves like a baby. "Daddy," I think, because I'm stubborn. Because he's been their daddy so long, his strong arms holding them in the water and out of it. Holding me too. It's hard to change, even though, I know, I know. You have to change.

I remember standing here with Jamie when he was three. I was pregnant and he was afraid of the water. I had to squat down so he could wrap his fretful little arm around my head. "Daddy is okay," he said, like a mantra, pointing at the speck of his father's head. "Daddy is a good swimmer and is okay." I rubbed his little velvet shoulder. "Daddy's fine," I said. "He's having a lovely time in the water. You'll join him again out there when you feel like it." I was so tired. "I will," he said thoughtfully. "I would like to." The following summer I watched from the beach while Jamie bobbed in the waves with his dad.

I shake my head now. Willa and Nick are clambering back toward us through the wavelets, the sun just a sliver of color tracing the water behind them. "Sunrise, sunset,"

I sing out, and Willa sings with me: "Swiftly fly the years! One season following another—laden with happiness and tears."

"And claaaaaaams!" Willa yells. "Oh my god, I'm starving!" And suddenly, I realize, so am I.